FINN

FINN

CHRISTOPHER BROOKHOUSE

SAFE HARBOR BOOKS
31 Page Avenue
Asheville, North Carolina 28801

LIBRARY OF CONGRESS CATALOGING-IN-PUBLICATION DATA
Brookhouse, Christopher, 1938-
Finn / by Christopher Brookhouse.
pages ; cm
ISBN 978-0-9798226-5-0 (acid-free paper)
ISBN 0-9798226-5-3 (acid-free paper)
1. English teachers—Fiction.
2. Man-woman relationships—Fiction.
I. Title.
PS3552.R658F56 2015
813'.54—dc23
2014021689

SAFE HARBOR BOOKS
www.safeharborbooks.com

FINN

ONE

"Finn, you always appear to be looking over your shoulder," she had said then in that lost time when I was lost.

Now she—Mrs. Spier, Providence Spier, called Belle by her husband, children, and everyone else—was dead, was in fact lying in the coffin surrounded by urns of lilacs, definitely not a local flower, which Belle was. Timon, her husband, who enjoyed being called "the judge," had predeceased her by three years, both victims of cancer—his lung, hers breast—he at seventy, she at sixty-six.

"You don't think someone's coming to take you back, do you?" Belle had continued.

"No ma'am," I answered.

Belle was a slender woman with delicate hands. In the lingering afternoons, she played the piano. Light gleamed on her wedding band, the only jewelry she wore.

When I was fourteen and took up residence on the upper floor of Judge Spier's house, Belle's hair had already turned gray. My mother considered her own hair red, though I, who to my embarrassment inherited the same color, think it orange, the shade of the pale carrots my mother grew in the tiny

I

garden near the empty chicken coop, where my father kept his stash of Mason jars. When the judge invited (insisted upon) me packing a suit case with my few clothes and filling a cardboard box with my meager possessions—mostly four volumes of the *Book of Knowledge*—to be transported, along with me, to the judge's splendid house, called Red Sticks, my father had disappeared years earlier and my mother had been gone for several weeks, leaving me alone with twenty dollars for food and rent. I had paid the landlord and survived on tomatoes I stole from neighbors' vines, and peanut butter and saltines that Mr. Dees traded me for sweeping and stacking goods at his market.

"Well, I tend to look over my shoulder, too," Belle had said. "Need to check if the messenger is trailing me. Of course he is. He's trailing us all."

"Who do you mean?" I asked.

"The messenger who tags us for the River Styx."

"Where's that?"

"My, you have a lot to learn," Belle said.

The messenger had indeed caught up with Belle. Father Chester placed the bread on my palm. Annabel, who had already drunk from the cup of wine, drew down her veil. Father Chester wiped the cup's rim before bringing it to my lips.

I returned to my seat in the family pew and picked up my prayer book, Belle's gift upon my confirmation. I sat at the end, next to Annabel.

We knelt (Annabel tugged up her black dress revealing the hem of a crimson undergarment), the prayer was spoken, we rose, and pallbearers from the funeral home lifted the casket. For an instant at the doorway of the chapel, they vanished into the light and reappeared on the sidewalk leading to the hearse parked in the shade of oaks, whose trailing moss swayed in the June breeze.

I followed the sisters—Annabel, Caroline, Delia—past the eyes of the mourners, pausing at the door to pat my jacket pockets for my sunglasses.

The funeral home had offered a limousine for the ride to the cemetery, but the sisters, often referred to as "the late children," preferred Delia's tan Buick. "Finn can drive," Delia said to the others as if I weren't there. But Delia had always treated me that way.

Delia was 31, three years older than Annabel, who was born a year before Caroline, and the tallest, her chestnut-colored hair pinned up in a bun like Belle had worn hers. Caroline was tiny compared to Delia, not much over five feet tall, dark eyes and dark hair. A pixie cut, she called it. She disapproved of the time and money that Annabel spent having her hair dyed blond and curled and cut, so that it fell abundantly to one side of her face, requiring her shapely hand to push it back, when she invited you to kiss her. Delia had piercing gray eyes. She disapproved of the way Annabel dressed to invite more than a kiss. Annabel's eyes were different shades of blue, depending on the light.

So I drove, the sisters seated behind me. Delia reminded them that Tracy Haywood, the family attorney, would see them tomorrow at his office at eleven to present the will.

"Any surprises, you think?" Caroline asked. Once she would have lengthened the syllables into sighs, but she'd spent time in London and preferred not to sound southern anymore. I glanced into the mirror and found Delia and Annabel looking back.

"Share and share alike, I imagine," Delia said.

"What about Finn?" Caroline leaned forward and tapped my shoulder.

"I'm grateful for what I've already received," I said.

Delia said, "Finn, you sound like a pompous little shit."

"Don't you recognize irony?" Annabel said. "He expects something substantial. Hard cash. Or do I mean cold cash? In any case, funds are required to support his life style among the disreputables."

I smiled. Annabel hid them behind her gloved hand, but I detected the sparkle in her eyes. Surely the red undergarment was for me. I wondered if her others were red, too.

Caroline sighed. "We shall all be rich then. Rich late children."

Traffic stopped. I followed closely behind the hearse as it passed Dixie Corner, the new shopping center, and, at the defunct Hudson dealership, turned up Greenway Road, which winds past the municipal golf course and ends at the cemetery. The proximity of one to the other amused the judge, several of whose friends had collapsed conveniently near the burial plots they had chosen with care, as if their spirits might gaze eternally upon those whose strokes were not, at least not yet, as fatal as their own had been.

I parked and opened the door to let the sisters out. All I lacked was a cap to doff and a proper uniform, perhaps one with jodhpurs tapering into puttees, the outfit Spud, the judge's handyman and chauffeur, used to wear. The summer after Truman's surprising victory, Spud had passed away. I was fifteen. Spud was going to teach me to drive. Annabel, who was seventeen, said she would do it. She taught me other things, too. I was twenty-six now, and I remembered all of them, not the purest of thoughts to have as I waited for the other mourners to gather at Belle's graveside.

The cemetery land is the highest in Blue County. I contemplated the town from a distance, the brightness of its steeples, the rose of its bricks. Sprite is not a large town, twelve hundred according to the last census. Cotton and peanuts are its major sources of income, though rice once was. The hospital is the county's largest employer, though the army once was. Then there is the Academy, founded as a military school in 1845—now no longer that—and held in such low regard that historians credit its graduates for many Confederate blunders during the War Between the States. The disreputables to which Annabel referred were my colleagues, whose disregard of manners and traditions had not endeared them to the community. We had admitted a student of the Negro race. We intended to admit more.

While Belle descended into the dark earth, Father Chester patted his face with his handkerchief. He offered another prayer, assuring us that Belle's soul, as ours, would rise into eternal life. Someone behind me expressed the hope that summers would be cooler there.

Delia stepped forth and opened her hand. The lily she'd been holding disappeared into the grave. Caroline and Annabel released their flowers, too. Then, from behind Tracy Haywood, who was standing next to Calvin Huey, president of the bank, a figure emerged and accidentally bumped the elbow of Miss Pitts, grand dame of the United Daughters of the Confederacy, as he made his way steadily forward. She beheld his face and gasped, much to my enjoyment. At the edge of the grave,

Henry Broken-ground looked in my direction, nodded, held up something that I couldn't make out, something metal that caught the light as he tossed it into the air and gravity pulled it downward to the flowers and the coffin and the freshly-turned earth. The sisters, as did the rest of the mourners, exchanged puzzled glances.

Annabel took my arm, and we followed Caroline and Delia to the car. "Are you coming back to the house?" Annabel asked.

"I'm driving, remember?"

"Smart ass. I mean you're stayin' for the party, aren't you?"

"Is it a party?"

"Farewell, I suppose." Her hip brushed mine. "But you and I could make it a party."

"What are you serving?"

"I told Asia to put out tea and punch, whiskey variety in the silver bowl, the rum kind in Belle's favorite pressed-glass one."

The sisters stood aside. I opened the doors again. They arranged themselves on the back seat, Delia the last in. She gave me a long, disapproving look, which I interpreted as a warning not to investigate the shades of Annabel's underwear, no matter how willing Annabel might be for me to do so.

We passed Dixie Corner. "I think I'll buy a new car," Caroline said.

"Do you really need one?" Delia asked.

"Something fun to drive. Something sporty and British. A Morgan perhaps."

"Where would you find one of those around here?" Annabel asked.

"I'd have to order it somewhere. Atlanta, maybe. Or I could go back to London."

"You need to stay home for a while."

"Delia, I'll go where I choose and buy what I want."

"With what?"

"With my share."

"You won't have it for months."

"Wonderful. I love London in the winter."

"Perhaps I'll join you. That dreadful Kennedy will probably be in the White House then," Annabel said. "But he is handsome." She tapped my shoulder. "Finn, you votin' for Kennedy?"

"Why ask?" Delia said. "When he's not beating the bushes for Negroes to apply to the Academy, he'll probably be beating the bushes for Kennedy."

"He hasn't been nominated yet," I pointed out.

"But he's going to be, isn't he? People say his daddy bought all the votes he needs," Caroline said.

"Daddies can be so helpful that way," Annabel said, cooling her face with the tiny Japanese fan from her purse.

"Well, I miss ours," Caroline said.

"I'm sure we all do," Delia said.

"What about you, Finn?" Annabel asked.

"He went out of his way to help me."

"He gave you things, but he didn't love you." Delia drummed her fingers on the red prayer book balanced on her knee.

"Delia, you don't know that."

"Caroline, you have no idea."

"Here's my idea," Annabel said. "A delicious, chilled glass of punch. Rum, I think."

"We're orphans now, aren't we?" Caroline said. "I shall have the whiskey. Wasn't it peculiar, what that Indian did?"

"If Finn had his way, that Indian would teach basket weaving or some such at the Academy."

I reminded Delia that his name was Henry. His sister wove baskets, which sold well to tourists. Henry would sometimes twine strips of leather into lanyards to give away.

I drove under the canopy of oaks and stopped in front of the house. Simon and his wife Asia worked and lived there. Belle had depended on them for years They had attended a private service the evening before. Now they came down the steps to open the door for the sisters. Delia told me to return the car to the garage. She wanted to tell me to get in my own car and leave, but that was going too far, even for her.

I detoured through the gardens. The camellias had faded; the gardenias were nearly in bloom. Naked, Annabel had loosed the flower from her hair, spread her legs, and placed it there, inviting me to inhale its fragrance. "Homage to a painting," she said. Monet's, I think. Annabel was home from her first year at college then, and, as she put it, "simply mad for art." Now she owned a small shop that sold art and antiques. The couch in the back room was quite comfortable, in case the mood should overwhelm her, as it often did on a rainy afternoon when, with a five o'clock highball in hand, Annabel would lament that Sprite felt adrift and isolated and doomed, and she felt randy and poetic. So why not languish in the pleasures of the flesh, she said, patting the cushions, biding me approach, setting down her glass as she reached for me.

Built in 1775, Red Sticks is a plain house with good bones. A major remodel in 1930 did not change the basic architecture. A wide hall runs through it, front to back. One half is called the kitchen side, the other the library side, though it is the great room that faces the row of oaks and is as far away as possible from the kitchen. From its windows one views the gardens and the orchard and the remains of the schoolhouse and the medical office. The original summer kitchen long ago burned. By 1900 the outbuildings were vacant. As Belle and Timon grew distant from each other, she occupied the master bedroom on the library side and he a smaller one on the kitchen side, the second floor accessible by the elegant front staircase. There are back stairs as well, and outside a set of wooden fire stairs, a convenient trellis for wisteria, leading to a landing and two small doors that were never locked, which, intentionally or not, allowed the coming and going of Mrs. Evening (the name Belle called her by) to occur without notice of her presence, other than the headlights of her Plymouth coupé when she arrived on moonless nights.

Tunisia, Asia's daughter, was seated on a bench in the garden, reading. She held up the book, showing me its title, *Native Son*. She was probably the only thirteen year old in the county reading Richard Wright. I was impressed. She asked me about Albert. They were friends. Albert was Albert Cates, the first black student admitted to the Academy. The announcement of his placement for the fall term was an item in the *Messenger*, our weekly paper. Erskine Purfoy, the editor, cautiously applauded the school's decision. Many felt otherwise. Three families had threatened to withdraw their children; two had done so. At Ruth's Café, an establishment frequented by Buckland Pickens, our sheriff, when concern over young Albert's safety was raised, opined that we should be more worried about the safety of those on the committee who voted to admit a black student. As he spoke, Buck looked at me. I, a young teacher, a man without the lineage of the headmaster or the older trustees who gave into the wishes of the younger faculty, none of them local except me, was more liable to receive threats than any of the others. I had grown up in Sprite and ought to know better. Even Belle, always kind to "the colored," a woman who spoke often of their race deserving better education, a woman who believed the decision a few years earlier favoring one Oliver Brown in his suit against a Kansas school board was an enlightened one, even she called me to her bedroom and, in breaths that were numbered, inquired if I thought I had acted wisely. I said I had. "You would do well," she said, "to keep watch over your shoulder."

"The messenger we spoke of once, and that river?" I asked.

She shook her head sadly, as if I knew so little. "I'm referring to water much closer to home," she said.

The body of a Massachusetts man, who stood one Saturday in the town square and handed out literature promoting Negro voting, had been pulled from Cane Creek.

"Miss Delia wouldn't like me reading this book, I bet." Tunisia raised the copy of *Native Son* from her lap.

"I don't think Delia reads much fiction," I said.

"But she knows what books she doesn't want in the house. It is her house, isn't it?"

"The sisters will probably all be owners."

"But Miss Delia's in charge now."

"Guess so," I said. "But she can't tell you what to read."

"Not directly," Tunisia replied.

About a dozen guests were gathered in the great room, punch bowls and pitchers of tea set out on a long table decorated with starched white cloths. The sisters stood at the door, sort of a receiving line. I assumed I was not supposed to stand with them. The urns of lilacs had been brought from the chapel and placed in front of the fireplace. Belle was fond of fires on winter evenings, but Timon was not. However, the great room was on her side of the house, so she enjoyed many fires. Wood smoke had darkened the wallpaper and the wainscoting and dulled the portraits of Landon and Calendar Spier, brother and sister, he a physician, she a teacher and nurse, who had survived alone the years the northern armies approached Red Sticks, but had not disturbed it. I assumed after Delia redecorated the master suite to her taste, she would attend to the great room next.

"Rum or whiskey?" Wilbur Cross asked. "Which do you prefer?"

Wilbur had the idea for Dixie Corner. Reluctantly the bank lent him money. Now that the spaces were leased up, except for the Hudson agency, those who once scoffed at the project had changed their minds, though many residents, who feared the Corner's success would draw business from the downtown, were still opposed.

"Whiskey," I answered.

"Not a surprising choice for a man whose name is Francis Finnegan Butler."

"You're right," I replied to Wilbur. "Whiskey it should be."

"What are you planning this summer? Write a novel? It is literature you teach."

"I leave the writing to others. I'm not sure what my plans are."

"You read *God's Little Acre*?"

"I have."

"You ought to write dirty books like that, or worse. With this Warren court, you could probably write pornography and get away with it. And get rich."

"I don't think I have Erskine Caldwell's talent. Not even Erskine Purfoy's." Erskine had editorialized in favor of Wilbur's project with more success than he had for Albert's entering the Academy.

"Mr. Caldwell shamed the South. People up north think he portrays us the way we are."

The sisters had moved from the doorway. Annabel was headed in my direction. Calvin Huey shook my hand and requested a moment of Wilbur's time. Annabel handed me another whiskey and took my arm, drank deeply from her glass of rum, and led me through the French doors to the porch. She leaned against one of the columns, as if posing there, her hand pushing her curls aside.

"Finn, do you think I need to lose weight? Caroline does."

"Perhaps you've gained a pound or two."

"Oh, Finn, I'm not wantin' to hear the truth."

I sipped my whiskey. "But in the right places, of course."

"Much better. Would you care to go upstairs? I think a little workout would raise my spirits. I'm certainly sure I could raise something of yours."

Annabel's capacity for pleasure, and her inattention to the time or place she sought it, never ceased to surprise me. I needed to be careful how I put her off. "Delia would raise hell," I said.

"You take the back stairs, and I'll take the front. She'll think I'm going to powder my nose."

"When you're not down in five minutes, she'll figure it out."

"What do you suggest?"

I suggested what would cause her the most inconvenience. "My place?"

"Delia requires my presence at supper."

"Nine o'clock?"

"Sweetie, rum now, wine at supper, and Delia will probably pass around that green stuff Belle was so fond of. Three or four toasts, and I don't think I'll be able to drive to your place and get there alive."

I'd run out of options. Nor was I completely opposed to fulfilling Annabel's wishes. The whiskey was weakening my resolve. I gave in. "The boathouse then?"

"Nine, or as near as I can make it."

Annabel turned to leave. I caught her by the wrist. I offered one more chance for her to reconsider. "You sure? I mean you just buried your mother."

"Delia told me when she visited that famous Paris cemetery, Pére Lachasie, she saw a bunch of prostitutes waiting for men leaving funerals so they could offer them comfort for their grief. It ought to work both ways. Women need comfort, too. I'm counting on you to be up to it."

In that lost time when I was lost, I had stood with my possessions at my feet, and the judge introduced me to the sisters as Mr. Butler. Delia, home from what she referred to as one of her "spells" at junior college, asked when I was starting to work. "His name is Butler, not his occupation," the judge had said. "Too bad," Delia responded.

I picked up my suitcase and started for the front stairs, assuming someone would follow behind me. "Daddy," Delia exclaimed. I stopped in my tracks. Simon appeared and gathered the box that held the books I had collected, and I followed him down the hall, into the kitchen, and up the back stairs to the servants' quarters. He set my books beside the cot in the corner of my room. I could hear rain falling on the roof above my head. "Mighty hot in the summer," Simon said. Tunisia was almost one. Simon promised she was mostly quiet. The only window was the dormer too high up for me to reach. The dirty glass scattered gray light around the room. Simon offered to find me a radio. I wouldn't miss my favorite programs, "Suspense" and "The Whistler."

I followed Simon downstairs to the library. I stared at the rows of books. The judge pointed to a chair. Belle came in. She asked me if I liked Ovaltine. She said she did. She always drank a glass this time in the afternoon. I told her I'd never tasted Ovaltine. "I suppose you've never tasted many things," she said. "But we can change all that." She smiled tenderly at me.

Belle closed the door behind her. I had the impression Delia was outside, listening.

The judge lit a cigar and blew smoke into the air. "I hope you don't think I've abducted you."

"No, sir," I answered.

"You are our guest. For how long, I am uncertain. As soon as your mother returns, you shall return to her."

"Do you think she's coming back?"

"Do you?"

"She didn't say."

"She explained to Mr. Dees that she was overwhelmed and needed to get away for a while. He was concerned."

"Do you know my mother?"

"I know of her."

"Did you know my father?"

"Tyrone, yes. He clerked at Bobbit's."

I hoped the judge could tell me more about my father. If he could, he didn't choose to.

The judge looked away and tapped his cigar against the rim of the agate ashtray on the table beside him, but I couldn't read his thoughts. Mine were about my father. He'd gotten a ride on a truck going to Wilmington. The driver had returned, but my father had kept going, maybe to California. Plenty of jobs out there. When the war started, I hoped my father was a soldier. I imagined him in a uniform with a bright patch on his sleeve. Perhaps one with a tank and a thunderbolt.

"Finn, I've made arrangements for you to attend the Academy. You have no objection, do you?"

I was stunned. I couldn't picture myself dressed in polished shoes, gray slacks, dress shirt, and a blue blazer, the uniform students were required to wear. I didn't own any of that stuff.

"No, sir, no objections."

"Concerns?"

"Sir, I don't think I'm qualified."

"You'll do fine, Finn."

Delia opened the door and set a glass of Ovaltine on a table just out of my reach. "When daddy's through with you, Spud could use your help. You'll find him in the garage. Use the back door." The judge frowned. "It's closer," she said.

Years later I was still using the back door. I left Annabel and the others. Tunisia had been summoned inside to help in the kitchen. In town I stopped by Ruth's Café. Erskine was sitting with Danielle, who wrote obituaries and sniffed around Sprite and the county for local news, which was mostly what prices crops were bringing and how the weather was affecting everything from apples to pecans. But she also paid attention to what was going on in the lives of people who just got by and used the *Messenger* to paper the walls of their shacks.

Blue County was dry. The whiskey and rum were purchased elsewhere, but we did have some excellent distillers at hand. Ruth's was one of the places you could sample their products. Tell Ruth you'd care for strong tea. You've been feeling puny lately and *strong* tea would set you right. She'd serve it to you in a brown mug and lay a tea bag beside it for show. The mug wouldn't be full. Half full was about what most customers could tolerate. Sheriff Buck would take a couple of swallows and chew some Sen-Sen before he got back into the cruiser.

Erskine slid a chair in my direction. "Danielle says you were taking orders today."

I smiled at Danielle. "I was helping out. You should have come back to the house."

"I was keeping my distance," Danielle said.

Erskine pushed his tea in my direction. Ruth came over and took out her pad, just in case. I ordered coffee and a piece of pie. "The boy needs a clear head," Erskine commented.

"Sisters have you working late?" Danielle asked. I nodded. "Let me guess which one."

"She needs a favor."

Danielle lowered her voice and leaned toward my face, her eyes flashing with amusement or anger, or both.

"Favor? Is that what she calls it."

"Favor," I repeated.

"I guess she got the first letter right."

Erskine choked on his tea. Ruth brought my order.

Erskine was watching us closely, wondering how much we were going to say. The only other customers in the café appeared to be listening as well.

I finished my pie. Danielle lit a cigarette. "What's up with Henry? I was surprised to see him at the cemetery."

"After Spud died, Henry sometimes did errands for Belle," I said.

"And he likes to show up at funerals," Erskine added. "Entertainment maybe. Never could draw a bead on him."

"Couldn't get him in your sights, that's what you mean?"

"Danielle, I mean that I can't figure him out."

"The old ways die hard," she said.

"What's that mean?"

"Sounded as if you wanted to shoot him, not understand him."

"The old language dies hard."

"It's more than that."

"Danielle, please don't carry on."

"Well, you did a good thing praising the Academy for admitting young Mr. Cates."

When Albert's name was mentioned, the couple nearby stopped eating and looked at each other, a man in overalls and a woman in a print dress.

"Let's not go on about that either," Erskine said.

The man in overalls put down his fork, pushed his plate of barbeque aside, and took out his pocketbook to pay his bill. His wife folded her napkin and stood up. Negroes offended them. People who favored Negroes offended them more. Danielle realized the situation. She reached across the table and squeezed Erskine's hand. "I'm sorry," she said.

"Things take time," Erskine said.

Danielle watched me finish my coffee. Ruth bussed the table the couple had left. She looked with dismay at the half-eaten plate of barbeque. "I'll be outside," Danielle said.

She was waiting beside my Ford, one of the postwar models with a grille that was supposed to remind one of a fighter plane. She wore to town what most women her age, nearly 30, wore at home: flats, jeans, and an old shirt, probably one of her father's, who had died when she was in college. The French cuffs were frayed. The links were pearl. She cut her hair shorter than any woman's in the country, or any I knew of. She didn't use lipstick, not during the day anyway.

The man who had left the diner watched us from his pickup. His wife had gone into Bobbit's, the dry goods store. A selection of straw hats was displayed behind the plate glass window. "Kiss me," Danielle said. And I did. Her mouth was soft and open.

"Now," she said, wiping my mouth with her sleeve, you can go to sleep having kissed two women in one day."

"You know something I don't know?"

"Annabel does kiss first, doesn't she? Or do you just get right down to it?"

"She kisses."

"Well today I got you first."

Danielle lit another cigarette and walked up the street to her car, nodding to the face in the pickup's window.

TWO

Mr. Polk had sold me a house near the end of Little Run Road, which wasn't paved. My house was scarcely more spacious than the trailers parked on Mr. Polk's other property, about a mile closer to town, but it was a roof over my head that I could afford, thanks to Belle's help. Opposite my house was a field of tall weeds where deer browsed in the evening. Mr. Polk wasn't much interested in farming. Renting property took less time and paid better. He had gone north to school and graduated from Mr. Jefferson's university, but he pretended to shun learning.

I parked near the gum tree in front of my house. I surprised a blacksnake, which slithered under the woodpile. I intended to do some reading, but I fell asleep on the couch. Later I cooked a pork chop and opened a jar of applesauce to go with it, and warmed up some of the green beans Danielle's mother had canned and given me at Christmas, six jars in all, decorated with red bows. "You need to eat better," she said.

At eight-thirty I drove to Red Sticks. The sandy path to the boathouse wasn't visible from the main house, but I kept my lights off anyway. I waited in the car. Sometimes that's where Annabel liked to be. My Ford had plenty of room and soft seats, though the cloth prickled a bit. We could feel the floor through the old mattress in the boathouse. It wasn't as agreeable as it had been when we were home from college and snuck away to pass a long afternoon together. The boathouse was always dark, and it seemed like night inside, appropriate for what Annabel called "in-and-out time," whose first occurrence had taken place in the station wagon Annabel used to teach me to drive, and which I was recalling, when Delia appeared out of the darkness and shined a flashlight in my eyes.

"You lost?"

"Just enjoying the evening," I said.

"Too bad you won't be enjoying Annabel." I could smell the alcohol on Delia's breath. "She did some imbibing. You know how she is."

"I know some."

"I know some, too." A revolver appeared in Delia's hand. "The sheriff feels like there's troubling times ahead, for women especially. He feels we're not prepared. He's been teaching some of us to handle firearms. I warn you, I'm a good shot, and you're on my land. You're trespassing. I'd hate to shoot you, considering we've lived in the same house together as if you belonged there. In the dark, though, a trespasser's identity can be as obscure as his intentions."

"Or hers," I said.

"Don't joke about your situation, Finn. Heed my words."

Delia switched off the flashlight. I couldn't see anything. For a while I sat in the dark. When I turned on my headlights, Delia was gone.

Tracy had requested my presence. I arrived at his office before the sisters. I declined the cup of Maxwell House that Miss Pickens, Tracy's secretary, offered me. The sheriff was her cousin. I sometimes wondered if she passed on confidential information to him.

The inner door opened and Tracy greeted me, calling me "Young Finn," which was the way Timon introduced me to people.

"Not so young anymore," Tracy said and shook my hand.

We agreed that Belle's service had been short and to the point, as Episcopal services are, not one of those kinds where people stand up and say all sorts of things about the dead, sad stuff and funny stuff and some too embarrassing to have been spoken at all. How Homer Stand, principal of the elementary school, had, as a young man, relieved himself too close to the electric fence on his father's farm and received a jolt of current that knocked him to the ground and turned off his urinary function for several hours was one story that came to Tracy's mind. I noted the smile on Miss Pickens' face as she filed papers and pretended not to hear us.

Then the sisters arrived. Except for the colors, their outfits looked alike—tailored, expensive, with wide belts, and hems just below the knee. Delia wore gray, Caroline beige, Annabel emerald green. Her necklace was emeralds, too. Delia had a black hat on. Caroline and Annabel didn't wear hats. Delia didn't bother to look at me. Caroline said, "hello." Annabel mouthed a kiss. Tracy escorted the sisters into the conference room. I wasn't invited. I sat down and decided to accept the coffee.

A few minutes later, the sisters reappeared, Delia first,

pulling on her gloves. She paused at the doorway to thank Tracy for attending to the details required to settle the estate. Caroline patted my shoulder. Annabel mouthed another kiss.

"Come in a minute," Tracy said.

He sat at his desk. The neat rows of law books shelved behind him seemed to serve more for decoration than for reference. The leather chair facing the desk was the mate of the one in the reception room.

"Nothing for you, Finn. The sisters share and share alike. I think they knew that."

"I didn't expect anything," I said.

"Really?"

"The judge took me in and educated me. That's a lot."

Tracy filled his pipe, but didn't light it. "'The Judge.' You realize, of course, someone stuck Timon with that title, and not out of respect, but that's what it became."

"Any idea who?"

"Don't have a name, but someone who thought Timon was too big for his britches because he had money and power and didn't have to sully himself with practicing law, even if that's what he studied. Timon had power and money, no doubt about it. And he did things you couldn't do anymore, like taking you into his house, sort of adopting you without going through the formalities. If he had, I suppose you would expect something. A dollar or two, at least."

"I'm not disappointed."

"There is one thing." Tracy reached into his pocket. "This coin, if you can call it that. It was in the family's lockbox at the bank. I saved it for you."

The dull-metal piece was the size of a poker chip, one side

stamped with a pine tree; the initials *S.C.* were on the other, along with a number. Mine was 7.

"Seven," I said. "Seven what?"

"Not sure. Good luck, though. Call it a good luck token."

"And S.C.? South Carolina?"

"Shilling Club." I shook my head. "Long gone now. A joint off the highway between one jurisdiction and another, tucked out of sight. It was still thriving when I passed the bar, but my daddy told me to stay away from the place. Popular with soldiers during the war. Beer and spirits were legal then. There were women imported from Charleston or somewhere, with a reputation of being extremely hospitable to strangers. In nineteen forty-four, I think, the military put the establishment off-limits, and it pretty much folded."

I turned the token over in my hand. I said, "Not a place the judge or Belle would go."

"Definitely not Belle, and I doubt Timon would, even when he'd had a few."

I had a doubt of my own, but I kept it to myself. Tracy escorted me through the reception room. He laid a hand on my shoulder, said he hoped, whatever it was for, that the token would bring me good luck.

From where I'm sitting today, I suppose it has. But an hour after I left Tracy's office, the opposite was certainly true. I heard the fire trucks. The dust from their wheels on the dirt road to Polk's farm had settled. Smoke hung in the air: my house was completely gone, burned to the ground, only the chimney standing. One of Chief Sweeten's men was hosing down the smoldering beams.

Danielle was on hand, shooting pictures for the newspaper. The firemen, all volunteers except for the chief, were taking off their gear, wiping their faces, and drinking water. Off to the side, Henry Broken-ground was kicking the scorched grass.

"Finn, I'm sorry," Danielle said. She snapped the lens cover onto her camera and fitted it into the bag hanging from her shoulder. "Seems extreme, doesn't it. You lose everything?"

I didn't own much, but I cared about my books and the painting. They were worth something, especially the painting, "my cock," Annabel called it, a spectacular rooster with raging plumage, painted by one W. Glenn, an itinerant artist who had stopped for a while in Blue County in 1866 on his way home to Mississippi from the war. Collectors were always sniffing around trying to find his portraits and animals pictures. Annabel said the judge promised her the painting back when she was "mad about art." Annabel sold me the painting, four hundred dollars down and a hundred a year, and let me take it home. Under the fowl's prideful eye, on a winter evening we could shut the world away, our naked bodies warmed by the heat from the glowing fire logs. I still owed Annabel three hundred. She wasn't going to be happy that the painting had gone up in flames. Later I sifted through the ashes and couldn't find a trace.

News traveled fast. Father Chester told me to acquire what I needed from the thrift store at St. James in Burke City. The smaller parishes sent what they collected there. Danielle drove me. Mr. Sill, who ran the place, helped me find some trousers, shirts, and a pair of sneakers that almost fit. I cashed a check at the bank and bought socks and underwear at Bobbit's store. Mr. Bobbit sold me a pair of boots at half price.

Mr. Polk invited me to move into one of his trailers. Danielle loaned me sheets, a pillow, and a blanket. We sat for a while on her porch not saying anything, her head resting on my shoulder. Her mother had died in March. Danielle lived in the house alone. It didn't feel like hers yet. Otherwise she would let me stay there—if I wanted to. But that was a question Danielle wasn't asking me to answer.

I spent the next day scrubbing my trailer, about as complicated a task as I could concentrate on. The trailer was next to Henry's. "You makin' out?" he asked.

He was a big man, two hundred pounds at least, skin the color of burley tobacco, brown eyes. His head was bald, except for a trimmed scalp lock. His voice was soft, and he spoke slowly, almost sweetly. Some expected him to talk like Tonto and thought he was a fake because he spoke like the rest of us. The white kids called him names, but they were afraid of him. People said they had witnessed deer come out of the woods, walk right up to him, and let him stroke their necks with his huge hands. He could snap a broomstick in half, bend iron, whistle a bobwhite from cover, charm a copperhead from a woodpile and dance with it, the snake dangling from his fingers. His sister earned money from her baskets. Henry did odd jobs, helping out here and there, but he didn't get invited much into people's houses. Ruth would serve him on the back steps of the café. At times he would disappear, becoming invisible in the landscape.

I was supposed to drive over to the Academy and fill

out my book orders for the fall. I intended to stand up and get going, yet I kept sitting on the wooden chair that the previous tenant had abandoned, along with some pots and pans. I wasn't ready to cook anything. Velveeta, crackers, and fruit were enough.

I was holding the token—maybe because it was one of the only things I owned that hadn't burned. I showed the token to Henry. "Seen one before?"

" 'Deed so. It's a claim check." He handed it back to me. "From that club."

I wondered what had gone unclaimed. "You were there?"

"Early nineteen forty-three. The army turned me down for being color-blind, and Miss Wilkes hired me to wash dishes at the club. Worked for her until she closed."

"Just washing dishes?"

Henry smiled. "I helped a bit at the house."

"House?"

"Back from the club. The girls stayed there. They was always needin' something."

Henry stared at me until I stood up and aimed myself toward my car and my car toward the Academy. I sat in my office trying to decide if I needed to replace the poetry anthology I'd been using. My office has a tall window facing the grass circle and the flag pole in front of Fletcher Hall, the school's original building, named for Patrick Fletcher, the old Indian fighter, who had distinguished himself against the Creeks at Horseshoe Bend. Rain was beginning to fall, washing the dust off my car, which was parked in the visitors' area, where faculty members were allowed to park during the summer. Commencement had taken place at the end of May.

Dr. Curry, the headmaster, knocked on my door. He looked at me and shook his head.

"Arson?"

"Probably. The sheriff is investigating."

"Because of Cates, you think?"

"The sheriff thinks so."

"So does Albert's mother. She says Albert has changed his mind. Could be worse."

"Worse than what?"

"I mean you could have been killed. Our neighbors don't wear sheets and burn crosses anymore, but there are accidents: a limb falls on someone's head, a pickup truck drifts off the road, a man drowns in Cane Creek. Massachusetts man. Can't recall his name."

"Danvers."

"Sounds like a Massachusetts name, doesn't it?"

"We have a Danvers family here."

"No kin, I bet."

Boone Danvers repaired mowers and small engines. His wife raised chicken and sold eggs. Boone did not mourn the fate of Tom Danvers, a stranger from Boston. "Must have took a wrong turn somewhere. Should have learned to swim," was the comment he gave Danielle when she inquired if he knew the victim. No, they weren't related.

"Look," I said, "I'm going to talk to Albert."

"If his mother lets you near him."

People called Ella Cates a "proper woman." To some that meant she bathed, dressed in clean clothes (usually a white uniform, because from September to May she worked in the kitchen at the county's white middle school), was polite, and spoke well (her mother had been a teacher at the black middle school). To others she was aloof or proud, and seldom went to church. Booker Cates, her husband, had fought in a segregated infantry division in Italy and returned depressed and ill. Soon after Albert was born, Booker died. Now Ella worked hard and dedicated herself to her son. She lived in a small house she'd bought with insurance money. She didn't have many neighbors. She kept her husband's car, a Chevrolet, twenty-three years old, but dependable. She was careful, I thought, not aloof.

I stopped in front of the house and tooted my horn. I could see Ella hoeing her garden. She glanced up, stared at my car, turned her attention again to work, then leaned on her hoe, realizing I wasn't going to leave before we exchanged opinions.

We stood by a cold frame, she on one side, I on the other. She pulled off her straw hat and fanned her face. It was lean and dark and determined. She would speak her mind, directly.

"I'm sorry about your property," she said. "Least you weren't hurt."

"I'd be hurt if Albert didn't enroll at the Academy."

"That's your choice. Albert's is to stay in the county school."

"Or is that your choice?"

"My son and I agree."

I looked back toward the house, the green boards and white shutters. Clothes hung drying on a line. Some banty chickens were pecking at the edge of the garden.

"I'd like to speak to him."

"He's staying with a relative."

"Far away?"

"Far enough."

We looked into each other's eyes for a moment. "I'd best return to my chores," she said.

The gate to Red Sticks was closed. No amount of horn tooting was going to persuade Delia to tell Simon to open it. I drove down the path to the boathouse, parked, and walked through the orchard to the house. I found Tunisia out back, reading. I had brought along a book to give her, a paperback copy of *Member of the Wedding* that I had in my car when the fire broke out. I'd bought the book to read myself, but having it along to give her provided me with an excuse to be there at all.

"I heard someone shot at you."

Delia probably hoped someone would shoot at me. "Hasn't come to that," I said.

I asked if Albert was visiting a relative, where he might be. Tunisia didn't know. Albert never talked about family.

I hadn't told Tunisia about my conversation with Mrs. Cates, but she figured out the reason I was asking. "There's bible camp, but he can't hide out there for long," she said.

"Am I expecting too much," I asked, "wanting Albert to change schools?"

"Too much of him or his mamma?"

"Either or both."

"She already lost her husband."

"I know Albert was excited about enrolling."

"Mr. Finn...Tunisia hesitated. She was a precocious thirteen going on thirty. She had thought about the situation in a way I hadn't and wanted to saying something, but didn't think it was her place to say it.

"Go on. Please."

"Someone might say nothing changes. You're still askin' a black boy to do your work."

I considered how to answer her. Delia appeared and stationed herself between Tunisia and me. "The book in your hand, you bring it for Tunisia?" I nodded. "Best give it to her and take your leave."

I laid the book in Tunisia's lap.

"I'm feeling kindly toward you today because of your troubles, but you know how my mood can change on a dime." I nodded again. If I'd worn a cap, I'd have been holding it in my hand, my head bowed. Delia continued, "I mentioned to Simon putting a gate across the boathouse road. Keep out the riffraff."

I nodded and took my leave. Passing the orchard, I saw Annabel on the river. When I reached the dock, she was mooring her boat.

"You look far too serious," she said. The top of her bathing suit had slipped down, and she let it hang loose. She liked to row the skiff into the middle of the creek, strip off whatever she had on, and lie in the sun. Her breasts were already tanned. "What happened the other night? I waited for you. I had to carry on by myself."

"Delia said you weren't coming."

Annabel laughed. "She was wrong. I was, and I did."

Sometimes the way Annabel talked bothered me. I was a bit of a prude. I'd never heard a woman say some of the things she said. On the other hand…

"Did you lose everything?" Annabel asked.

I took the token out of my pocket. "Just about." I placed the token on my palm and showed it to her.

"What is it?"

"A lucky charm?"

"Does it work?"

"Not yet."

"What about you?"

"I've got a lot on my mind," I said. "I'm not in very good condition."

"Of course your cock is gone."

It took me a second to realize that Annabel had changed the subject.

"Gone. Completely. Nothing."

"Very disappointing."

"And expensive."

"Money isn't the point."

"But I still owe you."

"There's the insurance. I'm sure we can negotiate—when you're in working order again." Annabel shrugged and her top slid lower. "Caroline's got the right idea. She's going back to London. Maybe you ought to go somewhere."

"You think burning my house isn't enough?"

"You're not some stranger. The diehards treat outsiders better than those born here. They may not be through with you. You should have known better." She smiled. "I'm not through with you, and I know better."

The café was empty except for Erskine, Danielle, and me. Ruth had given up straightening the salt and pepper shakers, sugar bowls, and napkin holders, trying to overhear our conversation. She'd retreated to the kitchen. Erskine was nursing his own cup of strong tea; Danielle and I were sharing ours.

I elaborated what I thought Tunisia was thinking: We should solve the problem ourselves and not send one of them to get harassed or shot or worse to even things out. It's our problem to start with.

"How old is she?' Erskine asked.

"Thirteen."

"Thoughtful."

"But not very practical," Danielle said. "One of them has to go first."

"And a child shall lead?"

Danielle glared at Erskine. "A child with a brave heart."

"And is Albert Cates the chosen one, the child with the brave heart?"

Danielle looked at me. "Is he?"

"I don't know," I said. "I don't even know where he is or if I can override his mother's objection and convince him to enroll as planned."

"Did you think it was going to be easy?"

"Danielle, I thought the faculty and the students, most of them, would at best welcome Albert, at worst ignore him, and we'd go from there. Small changes. The long, slow march. People get used to things, change their minds. Anyway, I thought Albert would be safe."

"Because you sent him to the field to do your work? *Our* work. He had our permission, so he'd be all right?"

"I guess that's what Tunisia meant."

Erskine finished his tea. "A lot easier," he said, "if Tunisia was a boy. She'd enroll. She'd do it."

A look passed between Danielle and me. Erskine was probably right.

I'd consumed my nightly Velveeta and crackers and a banana for dessert. I rinsed my plate and poured myself another Coke-Cola. "Hey," someone said. Henry was standing on the steps. I waved. He opened the screen door and closed it quietly behind him.

I offered him a Coke, but he declined. He scanned my surroundings and sat down in the other chair. "Bet you miss that rooster," he said.

I didn't think he'd ever been in my house. "When did you see it?"

"It was in the club when I started working there, hanging in the office. I'd see it every week when I got my pay. The look in that bird's eye, like he knew he was something to see and you weren't."

"How did you know the painting was in my house?"

"I gave myself away, didn't I?"

On purpose, I thought, but didn't say so. "I was never much for locking doors."

"Wouldn't matter. I got a way with locks. I know my way around them."

"You know a lot, don't you?"

"It's how I get by."

"Annabel said the judge gave her the rooster, but how did he acquire it?"

"After the club closed, there was an auction." Henry paused and shook his head. "No, he bought stuff before the auction. Private sale." Henry paused again to consider. "That's the way it was. The club was broke and everything left was supposed to be sold. Anyone could bid. But the man in charge let his friends bid on the best stuff before the public had a chance."

"Who was in charge, Henry?"

"Lester Tallmadge. A lawyer who lived in Burke City. Big ol' boy. White suit and a white mind."

I recalled meeting Mr. Tallmadge at Red Sticks once. I didn't remember what he wore. I'd never owned a white suit, nor wanted one. I had a white mind though, whether I wanted it or not.

"They rented a tobacco warehouse for the auction instead of having it at the club, because they didn't want folks at the property speculatin' about what went on there and who did it. There was a bunch of furniture and kitchen equipment, and towels and sheets and what not from the house. Mr. Tallmadge said the linens had been boiled for sure. No reason to think you might catch something."

"You buy anything?"

"I wouldn't have been allowed to hang around, except I was helping out. I stayed in the background, like a good Indian should." Henry laughed. "Like they thought a good Indian should."

I took the token out of my pocket. "You said this was a claim check. What happened to items that weren't claimed? Or were there any?"

"A few. Hats and umbrellas mostly."

"Do you remember if the judge bought anything besides the painting?"

"He could have. I think he and Mr. Tallmadge got into a disagreement about something. I was hauling a chest of drawers to someone's truck and didn't follow what was going on."

But Henry knew about the painting, and he'd come over to talk about it.

"I did some hauling for Annabel, too, when she moved into her store. Her daddy had let her have the painting. First thing she did was hang it on her office wall, and we stood looking at it, and she said, 'imagine all the things that bird has seen.' I assumed she meant events in general, the picture being so old. 'Makes me shiver,' she said, and she rubbed her arms like she'd walked outside on a frosty morning. But her body was warm enough. She stood right against me, and I could feel the heat. Maybe I shouldn't tell it, but I sure did. And she did, too. She knew what I was feeling, what she was doing to me, and she kept on and, well, you know. She asked me for one of the lanyards I used to make. I gave her one with a bear claw, the only one like it I ever made."

Henry hadn't wanted to talk about the painting, he wanted to talk about Annabel. And yes, I did know. She'd sat right next to me teaching me to drive, her hand on my thigh, as if sending messages to my leg when I should step on the gas or ease off the pedal. After I managed to go smoothly from starting through second gear a couple of times, I turned off the engine, and we sat in the car sharing a cigarette that Annabel had stolen from the pack on the desk in the judge's study. I never took up smoking, and Annabel quit after the judge was diagnosed with lung cancer, but Annabel never quit doing what she did in the car that afternoon, her fingers stroking my thigh. Oh yes, I'd felt the heat Henry felt, and I couldn't blame him for wanting to talk about it.

Tracy Haywood wanted to talk, or at least ask questions.

Ruth was famous for her peach cobbler, and Tracy was enjoying some when I stopped by the café. He'd hung his jacket on the back of a chair and loosened his tie. He wiped his mouth, pushed his empty plate aside, and sugared his coffee.

"I was remembering your mother," Tracy said. "When she was young, she was a fine-looking woman. Had a real sense of style. Unfortunately she didn't have the money to make much of it, but she could shine in the most unworthy raiment. Do you remember her that way?"

I said I remembered her going out a lot at night after my father disappeared.

"Finn, let me be truthful, your parents' marriage was not one made in heaven. It was doomed from the beginning. They both had roving eyes."

"And roaming feet."

"Are you bitter?"

"Not at all. The judge was a generous man."

"In his way, yes."

"He was to me. My mother never could have afforded to give me the advantages he gave me."

"Not sure he was generous to Belle. Another marriage not made in heaven, but she wanted him. Waited for him to sow his wild oats. But he never finished, did he? He was still sowing with another woman, so rumor had it."

"We called her Mrs. Evening."

"And Belle wasn't wounded?"

"I think she found peace."

"And you? You must have been wounded when your mother left you."

"I was."

"She wounded a lot of us."

"You?"

"Finn, you know that old Hoagy Carmichael song 'Georgia on My Mind'? Well Georgia, your mother, has been on my mind since I was home from law school and saw her working at a Christmas party at Doctor Spender's place, bringing food from the kitchen and passing plates of shrimp around. I was supposed to be courting Missy Spender, but I couldn't take my eyes off your mother. She was sixteen. I asked her how she was getting home and said I'd give her a ride. I kept a little flask of whiskey in my car. We parked near the mill and finished the whiskey. She was a honey."

I imagined there was more to that night than sipping whiskey, but I didn't want to know about it, or other nights, which there must have been for Tracy to feel so strongly about my mother.

"Anyway, Finn, I apologize for rambling on about Georgia. I hope wherever she ended up that she's had a good life."

"I hope so, too," I said.

"By the way, still have your good-luck token?"

"Hasn't worked so far, but I have it."

"It will, Finn. You keep after things, and it will. I promise."

Later, as I lay in the narrow bed in the trailer, I wondered what Tracy was trying to tell me. Then I asked myself about the token. He said it was in the Spier family's lockbox. So, as their attorney, he should have given the token to one of the sisters, not to me, unless he found instructions to do so, and he didn't mention any. He was honest and meticulous. He was in his fifties and a bachelor. I couldn't think of him being careless, and I didn't want to think of him being a young buck sipping whiskey in a car with my mother. I wondered where she had ended up and what she would make of me if she ever saw me again.

Finally I put on a shirt and trousers and sat outside on a bench at one of the picnic tables Mr. Polk provided for his tenants. After a while, Henry appeared with a jar of strong tea. I drank enough to feel tired enough to sleep.

THREE

I dreamed I was cooking a chop. The skillet was full of grease and caught fire. I threw the skillet out the window and the grass caught fire. I was awakened by Danielle knocking on the door. While I dressed, she toasted a piece of bread and tried to make coffee in the tin pot that came with the trailer.

"Eat the toast," she said. "We're going for a ride."

Ella's yard was a mess. The fire trucks had been there and put out the fire. The house was all right, but someone had poured gasoline over her garden and lit a match. The trucks driving over the ground chewed up what might have been saved. Ella had decided to go away for a few days, leaving the house open to air out as much of the smoke smell as possible. In Danielle's opinion, the fire to my house had been a warning. The fire to Ella's yard was a reminder. I had been burned out. She hadn't been.

Danielle put her arm around my shoulder. "What about a real breakfast, with real coffee."

"My coffee is real."

"But you can't drink it."

I mentioned the inn in Burke City. Thirty minutes later

we were ordering eggs and grits and real coffee. I could look outside and see the courthouse. Some men, who I guessed were lawyers, chatted at a nearby table. I asked Danielle if she'd ever met Lester Tallmadge. I spoke the name loud enough for the lawyers to hear it. They paused for a moment, then continued their conversation.

"Not in person. Erskine mentioned him a lot. You didn't get on the Democratic ballot unless Lester Tallmadge put you there," Danielle said. "Did you meet him?"

"He used to call at Red Sticks to visit with the judge. Belle pointed out his car to me, a Ford, but it had a custom body that you could order special from the factory. In general I wasn't invited to meet people who had business with the judge. Once, though, Mr. Tallmadge asked to meet me. He shook my hand, praised my grip, manly not weak was the way it should be, and told me to keep doing well in school and I'd end up making the judge proud. I promised I would."

"What are you thinking?" Danielle asked.

"I'd like to see him again."

"Considering running for office?"

"Not at all."

"Then why?"

"No reason, except connecting with the past."

"That's a very good reason. Can you be more specific?"

I took out the token, laid it on the table, and told Danielle what Tracy told me about the Shilling Club.

"Erskine spoke of it once or twice, with fondness. I'm sure it wasn't a place he took his wife. What are you trying to find out?"

"Lester Tallmadge presided over the liquidation of the

club's assets and property. I wonder what he remembers."

Danielle wasn't looking at me anymore, but over my shoulder. I turned around. The man had been listening. His seersucker jacket was open. Not many people his age wore suspenders anymore. His were green. I admired his style.

"Mr. Tallmadge's office is across the street," the man said. "He's there ten until noon, Wednesdays and Fridays. When he's in his old office, his mind seems to go clear for a while, but what he's clear about is what happened twenty or thirty years ago, not last week, or even last year. Whatever you want from him he may not be able to tell you."

"But I can try?"

"We all do," the man said. He nodded to Danielle, buttoned his jacket, and walked away.

"They're all over town," Annabel said.

She had pulled the poster from the telephone pole at the corner. REWARD for information as to the whereabouts of Albert Cates, Negro, 5 feet, 4 inches, approximately 110 pounds, 13 years of age. If you have knowledge of this person, speak to someone you trust. Your information will find its way to US. The REWARD will find its way to you: CIVILITY, ORDER, PEACE.

A noose was drawn at the bottom of the page.

"Distressing," I said.

"You know anything?" Annabel asked.

"Albert's mother sent him away, but she didn't say where."

"Has the Academy got another candidate lined up?"

"None I'm aware of."

We were talking in Annabel's office. The shop was closed for the day. I'd been to the school and finished my book orders and started to redo the shelf list of the library. Each member of the faculty is required to coach a sport or contribute in some other way, like selling supplies in the tiny school store or advising the staff of the student paper. I superintended the library. I noticed the hem of Annabel's skirt rising inch by inch as she crossed and uncrossed her legs, and the afternoon light drifted across the room.

She had recently acquired an Audubon from an early edition, a framed print of a huge flamingo. The print leaned against the wall, next to a lowboy that she purchased from an estate in the Piedmont. For someone so young in the business, she had a knack for knowing when old families needed money and had something worthwhile to sell. Widows were persuaded by the money she offered; widowers by the charms she seemed to offer. She sat in a chair upholstered in red velvet. I sat on a leather hassock, my back against the wall, a good position from which to observe Annabel crossing her legs again.

"You ever fooled around with a man?" Annabel asked. I shook my head. "But there must be people we know who have, who do."

"I suppose."

"Father Chester, I've heard rumors about him. At Belle's service, when he laid the bread on my palm, I was wondering if his hands were clean." Annabel shivered. "Makes you wonder, doesn't it?"

"Don't listen to rumors."

"Here's a fact. Caroline's got an English lover, someone with a title."

"Sounds promising."

"I hope not. It's a woman. Caroline told me, but she didn't confide in Delia." Annabel looked at her watch. "Right now Caroline should be in Boston waiting for the London plane. And here we are. What are you waiting for? Do I have to send you a written invitation?"

Ruth was about to close, but she let me join Buck and Erskine. She'd heard I hadn't been eating much and offered to bring me a plate of spaghetti and some bread.

Erskine, amused at what he called my dishevelment, poured some of his strong tea into my cup. The sheriff frowned, as if running *dishevelment* through his store of vocabulary, trying to figure out what Erskine was referring to. My clothes were a bit wrinkled, but everything was on straight, more or less, and right side out. Perhaps Erskine was being metaphorical and had my mental state in mind. I wasn't all that happy with myself, or myself with Annabel. I was relieved Danielle wasn't there. She has a bad habit of reading my mind.

Erskine pulled the poster from his pocket and unfolded it. "I suppose you've seen these?"

"I have," I said.

"Completely unnecessary and a waste of time. My deputy's going all over taking these things down. Not a useful way to spend tax payers' money," Buck said.

"One way to look at it," I said.

"Everyone knows the boy changed his mind about attending white school," Buck said.

"I think some people want to make the point that he shouldn't have agreed to attend in the first place," Erskine said.

"I don't think he ever wanted to. His mother decided for him. The way she talks. She's very forward."

"She speaks her mind," I said.

"It's how she speaks it," Buck said.

Erskine shrugged. My spaghetti arrived, with a piece of thick bread and a square of butter.

Ruth turned on the radio behind the counter. She'd rather hear Bobby Darin for the tenth time in one day instead of us. For two years, most any time you listened, Bobby Darin was singing "Mack the Knife" or "Dream Lover," and now "Beyond the Sea." Better than a couple of years earlier. How many times did we have to hear the Chipmunks?

"Son?" I buttered my bread and looked at Buck. "You have any idea where Albert Cates is keepin'?"

"None at all," I said.

"Well, if you learn something, pass it on. I think this poster business is someone having fun, but I don't want any harm to come to the boy." Buck stood. "Erskine, I'd appreciate it if you wouldn't editorialize about the posters. Don't stir things up. For all I know someone who wants the boy to attend the Academy could be behind the posters and is trying to put the community at each others' throats."

"You being a peace officer, I understand your position," Erskine said. The irony was delicate. Buck smiled. I wasn't sure if he acknowledged the irony, or didn't hear it at all, and was expressing his satisfaction that Erskine wouldn't write anything about the posters.

After Buck left, Ruth hung the closed sign on the door.

The "Theme from 'A Summer Place'" was playing now. For a while Erskine and I listened.

"Finn, I'm assuming you were truthful and you don't know where Albert is staying."

"I don't know," I said.

Erskine picked up the poster. "Peace, that's our reward, isn't it?" He folded the poster and returned it to his pocket. "In the end, I'm told, there is nothing but peace, peace and the forgiveness of the Lord. I wonder if any of this matters to him. What's your opinion?"

"It matters to us," I said.

Floyd Patterson regained his boxing title, the first heavyweight ever to do so. The Swede that Patterson knocked out was white and Patterson wasn't, which caused some lively debates among Ruth's customers, but the few residents of Sprite who professed knowledge of the matter figured that the Swede had been lucky his first fight with Patterson, and luck for a white heavyweight didn't stick around very long.

The Democrats nominated Kennedy, the Republicans Nixon, who was probably a bit more popular in our county than Kennedy, but hardly anyone would say so.

The summer moved along and Albert's whereabouts remained unknown. News reached Ella that some of her windows had been shot out, BB practice. "Kids," Buck said. He had an idea who they were and was going to have a talk with them. "Not much to do for kids around here," he said, meaning they weren't targeting Ella in particular. They just saw a house with no lights on and a trashy yard and decided no one lived there and a few panes of broken glass wouldn't upset anyone.

Ella, like many of her friends, trusted Danielle's reporting, thought she understood their side of things, trusted her. When Ella called the newspaper about the broken glass, Danielle promised that she and I would replace it and keep an eye on the house. Ella offered that I could stay in it if I wanted to. Might be more comfortable than the trailer. She planned on returning in August to look for work. The school had fired her. We assumed Albert would show up in August, too, a week or so before Labor Day and the beginning of public school.

"This couch appears more comfortable than what you sleep on in the trailer," Danielle said.

"Probably is," I said. "But I've gotten used to the trailer."

"I bet the trailer isn't helping your romance," Danielle said. She raised her eye and cocked her hip. She had on jeans and a T-shirt so tight that it didn't hide much. She'd caught me looking at her more than once.

"What romance are you referring to?" I asked.

"I forget. You and Miss Spier just get right to the main course. No romancing required. Sort of a business proposition."

Danielle wasn't completely wrong, but I put on my annoyed face anyway. In fact, I hadn't seen Annabel for days. She had gone on a buying trip, Mobile and New Orleans, and planned to visit a girl in New York she'd gone to school with. The theater strike had been settled. The shows were playing again.

I found a broom and was sweeping up bits of glass. Danielle was wiping off tabletops and straightening the furniture that Buck and his deputy had pushed around. "May I ask a question? It's kind of personal, but it's something I've wondered about for years."

47

"No time like the present," I said.

"Okay, how did you and Annabel...well, I know, or at least I heard, that Lord's Gulf Station had a machine in the men's room that dispensed what was needed if ..."

"Danielle, you're blushing."

"I'm just embarrassed with myself. You know what I'm asking. You and Annabel, you were kids. How did she keep from getting pregnant? She doesn't seem the type just to hope for the best. Or did she trust in the Lord?"

"How do you know anything happened when we were kids?"

"Spud's daughter saw you two in the back of that station wagon Annabel used to drive. By the way, you don't imagine you were the only one, do you?"

"I would have heard. Boys talk."

"I agree," Danielle said. "*Boys* do."

I understood what Danielle was implying. A couple of names came to mind, but I finished sweeping and paid no attention to Danielle, who was observing me, arms crossed, pressing her breasts snuggly against her shirt, ready to name names. I wasn't prepared to listen.

"Are you going to answer my question?" she asked.

"Spender fitted Annabel with what she needed." I knew Spender was one of the names Daniel was thinking about.

In another hour, we were finished and waiting for Mr. Buckman from the hardware store to measure the windows. He would cut the glass and install it. There were several framed photographs of Ella's husband in his uniform. Bobbit's sold the frames, which came with pictures of movie stars in them. Girls visited the store to kiss Paul Newman or Tab Hunter, boys to imagine caressing Natalie Wood or Kim Novak. Danielle clustered the photographs on a bookshelf, near a large Bible. She sat down with it on her lap.

"Oh my." Danielle had turned the pages, admiring the Doré illustrations, and came across a photograph: Father Chester, a few years younger than he was now, head adorned with a wig of long hair, posed in a satiny bra and corset, its garters attached to nylons. Pumps covered his feet, and a fur jacket his thin shoulders.

"What do you think?" Danielle asked. I didn't know what to think. Mr. Buckman's truck stopped outside. Danielle slipped the picture into the middle of *Revelations*.

Mr. Buckman finished and installed a new lock on the front door. Ella had lost the keys to the old one. Like many of us, she never locked up, but that was changing.

In Ella's ruined garden a few okra plants survived, their pale yellow flowers open to the sun. I'd brought some corn to throw to the chickens, but they had disappeared.

Twice I drove to Burke City to talk with Lester Tallmadge. The first time he was in the hospital with pneumonia, the second time at home recuperating.

The third time Miss Polis, the receptionist, remembered my name, an older woman who wondered what a nice young man like me wanted to speak with Mr. Tallmadge about. I had no reason not to tell her. She had worked in the office for years and recalled overhearing the young lawyers talk about a club somewhere nearby. When she got too close, the men changed the subject.

"Is Mr. Tallmadge available?" I asked.

"In body," she said.

I followed her down the hall. Her dress and shoes and stockings were nearly the same shade of brown as the carpet. The walls were adorned with photographs of the enlarged faces of former members of the firm, the thick frames suspended from wires attached just below the dark molding overhead. The brass nameplate on the office door said Tallmadge. Miss Polis rapped on the panel of frosted glass and opened the door slowly. A wide face with blue eyes and white hair stared at us, or maybe only at me.

"Mr. Butler would like a word with you," Miss Polis said.

"Oh, sure, sure," Mr. Tallmadge replied. The door opened all the way.

"Didn't leave off the mustard this time, did you?" he asked.

"Mr. Butler wants to inquire about the Shilling Club," Miss Polis said.

"Then you'd better step in." Mr. Tallmadge pointed to a chair. Miss Polis pulled the door closed. Mr. Tallmadge sunk into his desk chair, which squeaked when he leaned back. He was a big man and must have been bigger once. His suit—it was white— sagged around his shoulders. The revolver on the desk got my attention. I breathed in the sweet smell of gun oil.

"Cleaning my weapon," Mr. Tallmadge said. "Need to be prepared these days. Now, do I know you?"

"We met once. I lived at Red Sticks."

"Red Sticks?"

"Timon Spier's home? The judge?"

Mr. Tallmadge frowned. "Yes," he said slowly. "Yes," more slowly. "The judge. His wife served the best ham. I like mine with spicy mustard. Yes, didn't I ask you about mustard? What was her name?"

"Belle, sir."

"You don't look like the boy who usually fetches my sandwich."

"I'm not, sir."

"Then how may I be of service?"

"Years ago there was a business called the Shilling Club." I took the token out of my pocket and pushed it across the desk. "The club went out of business, and you were in charge of its property and assets."

Mr. Tallmadge's eyes opened wide, as if he was trying to see his way into the past, but it just wasn't there. I hoped it was merely out of sight and might come into view at any moment.

He picked up the token and studied it. Then he lifted it to his nose and sniffed. Then he nodded. He nodded several times. He smiled. "Oh, I was a bad boy," he said. "I tried to resist. I was married and too old for sportin' around, but they had some women there that could melt the habit off a priest. You think they wear much under their robes? Now the Mormons, I understand they favor some special kind of underwear. Lots of holes in it, more than a body requires."

"You enjoyed the club then?"

Mr. Tallmadge's attention wavered. He tapped the edge of the token on the blotter on his desk. The blotter was stained with drops of oil.

"All gone," he said. He swiveled his chair toward the

window. A pigeon had fluttered down and perched on the ledge. Mr. Tallmadge stared out the glass, but I didn't think he was looking at the bird as much as something beyond, something out there holding his attention, some dimension of himself, his consciousness, that existed in two worlds at once.

"I wanted to give Marlene a present, but I tried to fulfill my obligation and let others bid first. The judge gave two hundred. I knew if I said three, he'd go four and keep going. I let him have it. The judge always got pretty much what he wanted."

If? "What present did you want to give her?"

The chair squeaked again. Mr. Tallmadge turned toward my voice. The pigeon flew away into a sky hazy with humidity.

"Not sure now, but that Marlene was something. What she wouldn't do."

I understood about Marlene, but Mr. Tallmadge wasn't being too specific about the gift he had in mind, the mind he used to have. "Did the judge bid on something someone left at the club and didn't claim?"

The eyes that had been turned in my direction now gazed upon the blotter and the gun. "I've made a mess here," Mr. Tallmadge said. "The boy will be coming with my sandwich soon. I'll eat it and then it will be gone, like everything else." Mr. Tallmadge fell silent.

"I'll go see what's keeping him," I said.

Mr. Tallmadge opened his hand and found the token in his palm. He frowned. "This yours?" he said.

I took the long way back to Ruth's, passing by Red Sticks. I noted a gate now blocking the path to the boathouse. The main gate was shut, too. I wondered what Delia did all day, what she thought about, who she thought about.

I could see traces of the judge in Delia's face, and traces of Belle in the features of Annabel and Caroline. Caroline was always dieting and kept herself thin. Annabel didn't swim or row her skiff much anymore. She'd added a few pounds. Delia was about my height, five ten. I don't think she had gained a pound since I moved into Red Sticks. She liked to ride horses then, and once, before attending a junior college in Mississippi, she had carried on a secret romance with, Annabel said, a stable boy. Annabel claimed the judge found out and chose a junior college for her in a place that put a lot of distance between the stable boy and his daughter. Two years of higher learning were about as much as Delia could endure, and probably as much as Timon could, too, because Delia would stay in college a few weeks, come home for a week, go back, come home, go back, come home. The college charged him extra for Delia to have her way. The institution always needed money.

Delia lived in Paris for a while. By that time, the stable boy was forgotten. Since then a few young men had courted her, but she never seemed interested in any of them, according to Annabel, whose enthusiasm for men more than made up for Delia's lack of it. "Maybe I should invite ol' Professor Kinsey down here to do a case study of me," Annabel said. "I figure the professor is missing some good material."

I was wise enough, however, not to inquire about it myself. I was never in love with Annabel, and I didn't mind sharing. She was the teacher. Other students were in the class. I should have graduated and moved on. In a way I had, but I kept hanging around. There was a kind of security in knowing what to expect and what was expected, how to make the teacher happy.

While I ate the tuna salad Ruth served me, I replayed my conversation with Mr. Tallmadge, some of which puzzled me. I imagined he remembered more than he was willing to speak of, things he could have been more specific about. Perhaps I was paranoid. After I moved to Red Sticks, I often believed people stopped talking when I appeared, friends of the Spiers, as if I had been the subject of their conversation. Was it like that with Mr. Tallmadge, a reluctance to say too much disguised as a loss of memory because what he had to say involved me somehow? Or was I too sensitive to the possibility that someone might know things about Georgia and Tyrone that I wanted to know? They were always out there, somewhere, strangers in different ways.

I paid my bill and walked back to my car. The brick storefronts gave up the heat they had absorbed all day. The energy was almost tactile—you could reach out and squeeze it in your hand. The shops were mostly deserted. Another sleepy afternoon when the poor sought shade where they could find it, those better off went swimming in the river, or some much better off cooled themselves in the pool at the country club in Burke City, or stayed home in air-conditioning.

My trailer needed air-conditioning, or at least more windows. Henry and his sister were seated at the picnic table sharing a pitcher of Kool-Aid. Delia could shut the gates, but she couldn't close off the river. I had a boat ride in mind. All I needed was a boat to ride in.

"I know one," Henry said.

His friend Bib lived in a cabin less than a mile downstream from Red Sticks. I had drifted past it many times with Annabel. Often we'd see the wash hanging out to dry, overalls and shirts, but no women's things. Tubs, old bicycles, and odd pieces of furniture littered the yard. We'd admire a heron or an egret posed along the riverbank. Ospreys nested in a tall, dead tree. Sometimes a brown dog chained to a stake barked at us. The birds paid him no attention. We didn't either. Usually there was a boat upside down in the grass. Bib wouldn't mind us using it. He was passing a few weeks at the county's expense. Henry didn't reveal what Bib was serving time for.

The shadows lengthened. Henry's sister cooked some noodles and heated a jar of tomato sauce. Over supper I told Henry about my visit to Mr. Tallmadge. When I mentioned Marlene, Henry smiled. Oh yes, he remembered her. "She treated me real well," Henry said. "Didn't have to pay for nothing either. She'd never been with an Indian before. I probably spoiled her for the next one."

We finished supper. On the way over to Bib's, we talked about cottonmouths and alligators. Plenty of the former, but no one had seen an alligator for years. A moon was rising. I breathed deeply the alluvial, sulfur smell of the water, trying to relax.

"You just want to look, right?" Henry said.

I mumbled something that sounded like a yes, but wasn't. I intended to walk up to the back of Red Sticks and see what I could see.

The boat was homemade. Bib had dug out a cypress log, sanded down the rough places, fitted it with two narrow seats, and shaped the bow to a point, leaving the stern rounded. Henry found two canoe paddles under the porch. I told

Henry to sit in the bow and I'd push off and paddle stern. I was wearing thrift-shop pants and sneakers and didn't mind launching from the water. I realized when I almost tipped us over that he might have been more familiar with the boat than I was. With Annabel I was always the bowman. It was her skiff and I followed her orders. Henry was letting me be in charge. I sat down, paddled, and the boat began to move over the water.

We passed the abandoned rice fields, the delight of ducks and duck hunters. The weathervane on the boathouse shined in the moonlight. Henry lifted his paddle from the water, thinking I would, too, and we'd observe the house from the water for a while, paddling only enough to keep the current from floating us away. Instead, I guided us closer to the shore.

A few lights were on, and I could see the wavering glow of the citronella torches around the patio outside the kitchen. The lotion Henrietta had given us was keeping the mosquitoes off our skins, but they buzzed around us anyway. Lightning bugs blinked above the grass. Crickets cheeped. Henry turned and frowned just before the bow nudged land. I dug my paddle into the mud and pulled the boat parallel with the bank and got out, leaving Henry in the bow and a paddle in the stern with no one to use it.

Asia was sitting in a chair, Tunisia on the ground in front of her. It appeared that Asia was doing something to Tunisia's hair, then I realized that Asia's arms were around Tunisia as if she were sheltering her. Then I understood why. Backlit in the kitchen doorway Delia stood, gun in hand. She pushed the door open. I ran, the first shot whizzing way over my head. Not sure about the second one. The boat was spinning around in the water, a few feet from the shore. I dove and swam.

The third shot plinked in the water, close to me but not too close. "Goddamn, boy. Goddamn," Henry was yelling. Then he wasn't, because the boat turned over, and we were both holding on to it, kicking our legs, trying to ride the current away from Red Sticks. Two more shots buzzed over our heads. The sixth time Delia fired, the bullet tore into the keel, sending slivers of wood in all directions, one into my cheek.

On the way home we didn't say much. In fact we didn't say anything. In my trailer, I stripped off my wet clothes, washed myself all over, and put on a dry shirt and jeans. I didn't have any antiseptic. I cleaned my cheek as carefully as I could with soap and water.

I saw the glow of Henry's cigarette. He was sitting at a picnic table. Henrietta set out three bottles of beer and asked what happened. "Thought I'd check the home place," I said.

"You're on your own next time," Henry said.

I apologized. Henry nursed his beer in silence for a while. Then he laughed. "Miss Delia don't shoot as well as I heard she did."

I wasn't convinced. A revolver? That last shot was either lucky or damn good.

FOUR

In the morning Danielle knocked on my door. She'd already stopped at the sheriff's office to pick up the previous evening's incident report. The *Messenger* printed a weekly summary of them. Delia had phoned the sheriff's office about a trespasser. She had scared the man off. She couldn't identify him. I wasn't convinced about that either.

"You?" Danielle asked.

"Me," I said.

"You better have Doctor Spender take a look at your cheek. It's pretty swollen."

The Spenders had lived in Blue County for generations. They'd farmed, lawyered, run the post office, and sold feed and farm implements. Harrison Spender was the first one to practice medicine. Belle told me she and Harrison grew up together, but she didn't care for him and didn't tell me why. She saw a doctor in Burke City. Most everyone else had good things to say about Harrison. Belle called him Big Spender because he bought a new Cadillac every year.

Ned, Harrison's son, whom people called Stony, had joined the practice. He drove around in a Ford pick-up. I saw him a couple of times with Annabel. His truck wasn't in the parking lot, which was nearly empty. A slow morning. The girl at the desk said I wouldn't have to wait long.

I sat down and thumbed through a copy of *Life,* admiring some winsome photographs of Kennedy. Nixon didn't photograph well, but Cabot Lodge did: Nixon's running mate was tall and patrician. Harrison himself came into the waiting room, addressed me as "young Finn," and shook my hand, his eye scanning my cheek.

I sat on the end of his examining table, my feet dangling over the edge, the starchy paper covering the table crinkling every time I moved. Harrison studied my wound, his eye bulging on the other side of the glass magnifier he held in his hand, his breath redolent of coffee. The nurse handed him a pair of tweezers, and he removed some tiny fragments of wood and a speck of metal that must have been from one of the screws attaching the keel to the bottom of the boat. He held up the speck for my consideration. "Here's the culprit," he said. Stony would have called it the nigger in the woodpile. Like a lot of the older men, Harrison, whatever he thought in private, was moderate in public. Stony wasn't.

"You'll live," he said. The nurse swabbed my wound with hydrogen peroxide. Harrison seemed remarkably uninterested in how I acquired my injury.

Harrison told the nurse to give me a tetanus shot for good measure. He wrote a prescription for some kind of antiseptic cream. "Use it twice a day."

I took the token out of my pocket and asked Harrison if he'd ever gone to the Shilling Club. "Never went there, but I had a lot of business from there," he said. "Fights and the rest of it. Soldiers being soldiers, girls being girls." Now was not the time to imagine the young Annabel sitting where I was sitting, while Harrison discussed preventing the unwanted consequences of in-and-out time. But the thought crossed my mind. How uninterested was he then?

As I left the office, Stony was parking his truck. He strode toward me, his boot heels scuffing the pavement. He wore jeans, a fringed shirt, and a Stetson. He carried his office shirt and white jacket folded over his arm. In another life he could have modeled for a cigarette commercial. He didn't comment on my dressing, merely gave it a professional glance. "What you doing for fun since Annabel's been unavailable?" he asked. I shrugged.

"She's some gal, isn't she."

A statement not a question, I assumed. I detected a message in his smile, as if he knew something I didn't and knew that I knew he did.

Buck was waiting for me at the trailer. He noted my bandage. "Small price to pay," he said.

Henrietta had taken my dirty clothes and Henry's into town and washed them in the Bendix behind Sugg's, an old filling station converted to a store, where black people bought staples and took household goods to trade or sell on Saturdays. She'd hung the clothes out to dry on a line stretched between a gum tree and a pole hammered into the ground.

"The smell of the river's hard to get out of clothes," Buck said.

"I like the smell," I said.

"Well, I don't like you trespassing."

"Didn't see my name in the report."

"I left it out. Professional courtesy. You ought to thank me."

"Won't happen again," I said.

"And your injun friend?"

"Wasn't his idea."

"Too many folks being led astray these days. People ought to know better."

"Which ones? The people who are being led or people doing the leading?"

"Finn, the judge may have taken you in, but your pedigree isn't so worthy that I would think twice about sitting your ass in one of my cells while I write up my investigation of Miss Delia's complaint. I tend to take a long time with paperwork."

"I don't think I'd like a cell," I said.

"Stay out of trouble, Finn."

After lunch, my cheek didn't hurt anymore. I peeled off the bandage, applied the cream Harrison had prescribed, and decided not to put the bandage back on.

I spent the afternoon at school sitting in meetings. Albert's whereabouts were still unknown. If we were going to recruit more black students, the coaches voiced their preference for ones with athletic ability. Albert had a big vocabulary and could probably play chess, but the school didn't have a chess team, just football, baseball, and basketball. The football coach argued that the town might not make a fuss if a black kid enrolled and helped the team have a winning season, which hadn't happened in a dozen years.

By the time I arrived, Ruth's was clearing out. Danielle

and Erskine occupied their usual table. I ordered a basket of hushpuppies with my strong tea. Erskine inquired about my boat trip. What, exactly, did I have in mind, other than minor criminal activity?

I explained that I didn't like gates and fences. I was going to show Delia that she couldn't keep me out. "Son, let her be," Erskine said. "That part of your life is through."

Ruth brought the hushpuppies. Danielle reached across the table and slipped her fingers between mine. "Finn, is that your supper?" I said it was. "No," she said. "I have something better." Erskine tried not to grin.

I followed Danielle to her house. She lived on Piney Road. Her father had sold insurance and farmed a couple of acres in his spare time and raised chickens. After he died, Danielle's mother got rid of the chickens and their coops because snakes had taken them over. She sold her husband's red Farmall tractor and let the fields spring up in weeds, which she paid someone to mow a couple of times a year.

Danielle had given away or sold most of her parents' furniture and installed new appliances. Kitchen, front bedroom, back bedroom, sitting room, and sewing room were freshly painted in colors much brighter than any her mother would have chosen or approved of. Danielle had converted the sewing room into a tiny office. Notes and clippings were tacked to a corkboard, along with a photograph of us, a Polaroid taken by a friend of Danielle's from college, Danielle and me leaning against a car, our arms around each other.

Cold roast pork, potato salad, green beans, and melon for dessert. "Better than hushpuppies," I said.

We shared a bottle of wine. Although Blue County had

elected to become dry again in 1947, beer was always available, but wine of any kind wasn't. Danielle had brought back a case from Charlestown.

Danielle had considered air-conditioning, but ran out of money. Ceiling fans were good enough. Tonight the windows were open and a cool front was passing through. We didn't need a fan. We sat at the kitchen table and sipped our wine. An owl hooted from the trees beyond the field, which needed mowing again.

"You look tired," Danielle said.

"I am."

She set down her glass, stood up, and swung her legs over mine, settling onto my lap. We kissed for a while. "You don't feel too tired to me," she said.

"I'm reviving."

"I'm aware you are."

She eased off my lap, and I followed her into her bedroom. She had painted the walls blue. The old color was pink. The old bed was narrow. The new one wasn't.

Later we lay side by side, holding hands. "Ella's back," Danielle said. She had met Ella at her house and given her the new door keys. Ella wouldn't lose them this time.

I didn't sleep over. Neither of us was ready to take that step yet. I had to pass through town on my way to the trailer. Someone had painted out the R in the sign. Now it read Welcome To Spite.

In the morning Danielle and I met at the paper and drove to Ella's together. Danielle had seen the sign. She was sure

Buck or his deputy would be out asking questions, checking on all those with criminal pasts. I'd better prepare my alibi.

Ella welcomed us. Her windows were repaired. Except for the yard, everything was clean and neat. She'd harvested a few okra and zucchini. She brewed fresh coffee, and we sat on the porch drinking it.

About Albert and all the fuss, Ella wasn't concerned. Albert was fine. He'd be home in time to start school. She'd lined up a couple of house cleaning jobs. She would be all right. Albert would, too. She thanked us for taking care of her property.

The Academy and the county schools would start soon. I didn't ask which one Albert planned to attend. I assumed I knew and wasn't going to change anyone's mind.

I mentioned that Danielle and I had admired her Bible, especially the pictures.

"Any you like best?"

Danielle shot me a hard look. "None in particular," I said.

A siren wailed, then another. "I need to see what's happening," Danielle said. Her tires screeched on the pavement. The sirens had almost faded into the distance.

"Out near your old place," Ella said. She meant Red Sticks.

I finished my coffee and waited for Ella to finish hers, hoping she'd give me a ride back to the paper where I'd left my car.

"There was one picture," I said. "Not exactly an illustration, though I suspect it must illustrate something, just not something of a biblical nature. Human nature, I suppose."

"Mister Finn, what are you talking about?"

"A photograph."

"Of what?"

"Father Chester, in his earlier years, a poignant moment."

"And I have this photograph?" I nodded. Ella shook her head. "Only pictures I got are some of my husband and Albert."

"We found it tucked in the Bible."

I followed Ella inside. She took down the Bible and opened it. Scanning the pages, she discovered the photograph. She held it close to her face, then at arm's length. She found her eyeglasses in her apron and examined the picture again.

"Gracious, that is Father Chester."

"No doubt about it."

"Poor man. Needin' to dress like that and needin' to do other things, must not be easy for him."

"There's always been rumors."

"There always are."

"May I keep the picture?"

"You think someone's going to tell you something?"

"I'm going to ask."

"Mr. Finn, you goin' to talk with Father Chester? He's delicate. Even when he was younger, he wasn't strong, not inside. You understand what I mean?"

"I didn't realize you knew much about him."

"I helped sort and mark things for the thrift shop that Saint James runs in Burke City. Father Chester would bring stuff over, and we'd talk. He seemed to need to."

"About anything in particular?"

"Just what people being polite talk about—crops, weather, who died, who got born. This and that. But I felt like he was talking around what he really wanted to talk about."

"Which was?"

"Himself. Isn't it what most of us want to talk about?"

I took Ella's reluctance to offer me a ride as a message to keep away from Father Chester. I set out on foot. About a half mile toward town, Henry appeared in Henrietta's car. Danielle had asked him to fetch me. He'd heard the sirens and done what Danielle had done, what several other residents had done, driven around to find out what was going on. At least it was Danielle's job to report things.

The sirens led to Red Sticks. Delia had shot at another intruder. She hadn't missed this time. The victim was Billy Poe. Po' Billy, people called him. He referred to himself as a handyman. Not many people trusted the quality of his work. Recently Stony Spender had hired him to paint his garage. Late in the afternoon, after the clinic was closed, people said they saw Stony and Billy sitting under a tree near the garage, drinking beer together. Danielle said she wondered what they talked about. Who died, who got born, this and that?

By noon we knew that Billy had died in the ambulance on the way to the county hospital. People said that he carried a Bowie knife, but no one knew that for sure. The size of the knife became more menacing as the afternoon wore on.

We knew Billy's body had been recovered from the bottom of the stairs. He had fallen halfway down after being shot. Self-defense, no doubt about it, we decided. Apparently Buck agreed. Before dark he drove Delia home. He asked Danielle to go with her, make sure she was settled down. Big Spender had sent over some sleeping tablets.

Ruth kept the café open. Erskine and I were sharing strong tea when Danielle arrived. In a few minutes we had the place to ourselves. Ruth poured Danielle a mug of coffee and turned off the radio so we could have quiet, and so she could hear what we said, while she cleaned the counter and bussed the dishes, mostly coffee mugs. Her customers had been drinking a lot of coffee while they offered theories about the event at Red Sticks.

Erskine pointed out that Danielle hadn't stayed with Delia very long. "Ella showed up," Danielle said. "Delia seemed more comfortable with her than me. Truth is, she didn't need either of us."

"What about Asia and Simon?"

"They're visiting out of state."

Danielle had already gone to the paper and typed her story. She confirmed what we heard or knew. Billy had snuck onto the property and into the house. Delia was upstairs washing off after weeding some flowerbeds. She heard the front door close. She got her gun. Billy was on the stairs. He had a knife. He said he was tired of people like her. She needed to learn her lesson. She shot him."

"I guess he learned his," Erskine said.

"So how are you?" Danielle asked me. Ruth had heard enough and had stopped refilling the sugar bowls. The kitchen door swung shut.

Confused, I thought, but didn't say so. I set my cup of tea in front of her. I wondered what Billy knew about Delia that set him off. Ella's going to Red Sticks bothered me, too.

"Delia phoned Annabel. She's on her way home from New York, or wherever she is." Danielle's expression changed as she spoke. Annabel should stay away. From the darkness in Danielle's eyes, that's what I wanted to believe she felt about Annabel, because things between Danielle and me didn't feel so casual anymore.

Delia's story added more confusion. I'd never seen her weeding anything. Simon's nephew tended the grounds, unless Delia had fired him, and I doubted she had. Second, from upstairs, unless you were already standing by the stairs, it would be difficult to hear someone shut the front door. It was too far away. And it was probably open already to let air in. The screen door would have been latched. Of course Billy could have used his knife to cut the screen or lift the latch. But Delia said she heard the front door open. According to Danielle, Delia, her bathrobe flying apart, snatched up her gun from a chair around the corner and came back firing—two shots, both to the chest. The image of Delia, her long legs, and perhaps more, revealed under her loose robe, gun in hand, was like the cover image of one of the Spillane novels that half the town's literate people passed around, so they wouldn't encourage such writing by buying their own copies.

"Did you see Tunisia?"

"She's there."

I had known Delia to prepare food, so I didn't wonder how Delia was managing without Asia.

Ruth pulled down the shades. Erskine settled the bill. Danielle and I stood by her car and watched Erskine walk past Bobbit's to his. "Thanks for last night," Danielle said. "Let's do it again sometime."

"Soon," I said, and kissed her.

Father Chester was sitting in the garth, reading last week's *Messenger*. The new one would go to press in another hour or so.

He looked over the paper at me. "Young Finn, my word, surprised to see you here."

"I've been arguing with myself whether I should be here at all."

"I've been having that conversation for years. Truth is, I have nowhere else to go. My sister would have me, but she's kind of bossy and I'd feel like I was eleven again. Sometimes I think I should go, turn things over to new blood, but I've been here almost all my pastoral life. I guess I'm waiting for the bishop to tell me to retire before I choose to. I'm sure some in the parish would prefer that day come sooner rather than later. That isn't your errand, is it, to give me the boot?"

"It might be easier."

"Easier, you mean, than what words you bring me on your own?"

"Not exactly words, Father."

"Oh?" He removed his glasses, breathed on the lenses, and wiped them with his handkerchief. "Something I need to see?"

I took the photograph out of my pocket. He laid the photograph on his knee and carefully returned his glasses to his face, delaying looking at the picture, as if he sensed what it was.

He held the photograph to his eyes and examined it. He nodded and smiled.

"I'm not here to embarrass you," I said.

"That would be hard to do. I think I'm quite lovely in this outfit. Mind you, once I was dreadfully concerned what people would think if they saw this. It disappeared from my office library several years ago. I concealed it in Breasted's *Survey of the Ancient World*. One day it wasn't there. Very puzzling. Where did you find it?"

"In a Bible in Ella Cates' house."

"Quite extraordinary. She worked at our thrift shop in Burke City, but never here, for me."

"I don't think removing the picture is something she would do."

"I don't either."

"Did you suspect anyone?"

"Mrs. Twain, the church secretary was the only person who had access to my office if I wasn't there, and a cleaning lady, Mary Peters. She was slow, in her head I mean, but honest as the day is long. She wasn't a person who would go snooping through books. I think she was kind of afraid of them. She couldn't read. Once she told me she dreamed that an enormous volume fell on her and broke every bone in her body."

"Mrs. Twain?"

"Gracious no. A sweet woman. If she'd seen me in this outfit, she'd have resigned and probably fled the county."

Father Chester looked at the photograph again. "Silver fox, I think. Not a garment many people own here. The label in the lining said Indianapolis. Cold winters up there. More people would have use for such a jacket. Here I imagine the owner was just showing off."

"How did you get it?"

"Someone left it in our give-away box, probably in the dead of night. The jacket was there in the morning. I always check first thing. Sometimes people drop off dead animals or trash, a sad commentary on some of the citizens. I intended to give the piece away, but—well, the evidence is in the photograph, I have what many would call a…" He paused. "Weakness would be the kindest name they'd give it." He paused again. "I still have the jacket. A sad commentary on me. In fact, I'd forgotten about it. Certainly now is the time to do what its donor intended and send the contribution to the store in Burke City."

"I'd be pleased to take it myself," I said.

"Perhaps we could trade, the jacket for the photograph, a remembrance of things past."

The jacket was in a box in the basement. The local soil was always damp and the church had one of the only basements around. A few minutes later Father Chester handed the jacket to me. The fur smelled moldy and the lining was torn, but it was certainly worth money to someone.

"Delia Spier," Father Chester said.

I thought he was asking about the event at Red Sticks. "Self-defense the sheriff thinks." Father Chester squinted at me. "The shooting? Billy Poe?"

Father Chester waved his hand as if he was shooing away a fly. "No, no. In the summer, the altar guild used to have girls from good families come and help set out flowers and tidy up and address envelopes for Mrs. Twain, things like that. Long time ago. Probably Delia was sixteen. She could drive here."

"Was she interested in ancient history?"

"She didn't seem much interested in books at all."

"What interests did she have?"

"She was spiritual, and she liked ritual very much. She used to attend the Wednesday morning service. It's mostly ritual, no hymns, a brief homily, communion, prayers. You'd know, or would, if you ever attended."

"Yet another sad commentary," I said.

"One thing I remember: the Sugg's boy, Leonard I think, the one who runs the store now. He used to cut grass here when he was a little older than Delia. She'd try to get him to attend the service with her, but he wouldn't do it. They used to sit here and talk. Don't know what about. Kind of sweet, black boy and white girl sitting and talking, like they lived in the same world. It moved me. It still does."

I stood up with the jacket and turned to leave. Behind me Father Chester said, "Finn, what moves you?"

I didn't answer him. I didn't know what to say. Another sad commentary to add to the list.

I spent the afternoon filling out more forms for the insurance company. My claim from the fire was modest enough, but they were reluctant to pay me. The value of the rooster was an issue, and so was proof of ownership.

Late in the day Henrietta knocked on my door. Henry had driven into town. When he was ready to come home, one of his tires was flat. So was his spare. She wondered if I could fetch him.

I bought a newspaper at the drugstore. Henry read Danielle's report out loud. Nothing in it she hadn't told us. Henry turned around to toss the paper onto the backseat. The silver fox jacket was there. He folded it on his lap and ran his hand back and forth across the pelts while he stared out the window, but he wasn't seeing the road, not the one in front of him.

"You remember me telling you about the stuff from the club in the warehouse. I saw this jacket, or one like it." He lifted the jacket to his face and smelled the fur. "Someone should have taken better care."

"It's been in a basement."

I told Henry that Father Chester had found the jacket in the give-away basket and I was taking it to the thrift store in Burke City.

Henry turned the jacket inside out and read the label: Elite House, Indianapolis. "Shawnee country," he said. "Ancient brothers of mine." He stroked the fur again. "Indianapolis. It's the same jacket all right. Smooth on the outside, smooth on the inside. Silk, you think?"

"Think so," I said.

Miss Polis smiled up at me. We chatted awhile. She'd heard about the shooting. So had Mr. Tallmadge. He remembered the judge had a daughter named Delia. I hoped he would remember me talking to him a few weeks ago.

He shook my hand and I showed him the jacket. "I didn't order that," he said. Not a good sign.

"But you may have wanted it, a long time ago." I laid the garment on his desk.

His chair squeaked. He leaned forward. "Did I say I did?"

"Remember Marlene? You spoke about her when I was here before. You wanted to buy Marlene a present. There was an auction in a warehouse and you saw something Marlene would like, but your friend the judge wanted it more. Remember?"

"He wasn't my friend."

"But Marlene was."

The gun didn't need oiling today. It was tucked away someplace. The stained blotter had been replaced. Mr. Tallmadge spread his hand over the fresh one. "She was more than that," he said.

"And you wanted to buy her a present."

"A fur piece. Nice one."

"This one?"

"Let me see."

I picked up the jacket and handed it to him. "Better than this one. This has an odor."

"It's been in a damp basement."

"The judge put it there?"

"Someone else."

Mr. Tallmadge lifted the lapels apart and looked at the lining. "Indianapolis."

"Yes sir, Indianapolis."

"Spender used to send his girls there. But Marlene never had to go. She could take care of herself."

"Harrison Spender?"

"Doctors shouldn't ride around in Cadillacs. Makes people think they're getting rich off them." Mr. Tallmadge pushed the jacket toward me. "Shame to let something get ruined that way. Marlene wouldn't have let it happen." He turned his chair to the window and sighed. "All gone," he said. "All gone."

I thanked him for his time. I think he heard me, but he kept looking out the window.

The thrift shop was a block from the church. I parked by a loading lock. Someone had left a vacuum cleaner and a box of books. I read the store hours on the sign on the door: open now only on weekends for the rest of the summer. But the door was unlocked. Inside two ladies were seated beside a pile of clothes and a box of hangers. Mr. Sill set down a lamp. "You're back." He reminded me I could shop on Saturday. I told him that Father Chester wanted me to make sure he received the jacket. I handed it to him.

"How is the Father?"

"Well," I said.

Mr. Sill held the jacket up, shaking his head. One of the women came over and they discussed how much a furrier would charge to bring the fur back to life, so to speak.

I was halfway to my car when Mr. Sill called after me. He trotted across the parking lot, his arm raised above his head. "We get lots of coats and jackets with holes in the pockets. I always check around to see if anything fell through. I found this." He handed me a key.

FIVE

I intended to ask Henry what he knew about Dr. Spender sending girls to Indianapolis. Henrietta appeared at the door of her trailer. Henry was in jail. She didn't know why, only that he'd hitchhiked to town for the car and Buck had arrested him. Danielle had brought her the news. I went looking for Danielle at Ruth's.

"Expired drivers license," Danielle said.

Meatloaf was the special. "A couple of servings left," Ruth said, when she set down Danielle's coffee.

Meatloaf was too filling for a late lunch. I ordered a ham sandwich instead, and ginger ale.

"Buck can't keep Henry in jail for an expired license," I said.

"Buck can pretty much do what Buck wants."

"I don't see the point."

"Control, Finn. Buck's making a statement."

"More like a warning."

"Exactly. To anyone who might cause trouble, or anyone Bucks thinks might be thinking of causing trouble."

"People he's afraid of?"

"I wouldn't express that point of view to Buck."

I finished my sandwich. Danielle and I stood outside by my car. I noticed the shades of Annabel's shop were raised. I could see her on the other side behind the window, arranging a display of chairs. She could see us, too.

Danielle kissed me. "I'll be home all night," she said.

After dark Henry appeared at my door. Buck had set him out at the town limits. The welcome sign had been removed. The highway department would send a replacement. Wouldn't take long.

"Good walk always works up the appetite," Henry commented. Henrietta was cooking him supper. "Thirst, too."

I opened two beers and we sat outside drinking them. The smell of fried chicken drifted from Henrietta's trailer.

"Indianapolis. Lester Tallmadge mentioned how Doctor Spender used to send girls there. Know about that?"

"I heard of it."

"Pregnant girls?"

"Not when they came back."

Henrietta brought out a platter of chicken, a bowl of coleslaw, and a plate of biscuits. I opened more beer, three this time. She offered me a drumstick, but I knew Henry wanted it. I settled for a breast and a wing.

Henry told his sister about the jacket I'd taken to Burke City. Henrietta wondered why someone would give something like that away. I mentioned the key. I took it out of my pocket. Henry held it up to the slant of light from the trailer window. "Looks like most keys," he said. "Ain't been used for a while."

I knew him well enough to suspect he had an idea about something he didn't want to reveal, at least not yet.

After we finished eating, Henrietta carried the dishes back to the trailer and I opened more beer. "Buck's a hard man," I said.

Henry took a long swallow and grinned. "I'm a lucky man," he said. He fished a cigarette out of his pocket. "Buck doesn't know about my visit to the doctor."

"Which one?"

"Stony. His garage has a nice new coat of paint."

"You went to his house?"

"Sneaked through the woods, like one of my people spying on the Long Knives. Took a while for Stony's wife to leave. She usually drives off around eleven to shop."

"Long Knives?"

"Your people."

"Stony wasn't there either?"

"Course not."

"Why were you?"

"Miss Annabel stores stuff in the garage, things she buys and hasn't room in the shop to put them, or pieces she's going to send to the man in Burke City who refinishes furniture. I've helped her unload before."

"There must be plenty of space at Red Sticks."

"Delia objected."

"Were you looking for something specific?"

"Just looking."

"And if you got caught, you'd just be looking at yourself behind bars for a long time."

"Told you I was lucky." Henry finished his cigarette. "So are you."

"I'm lucky?"

"She has the painting."

"The rooster?"

"Wrapped up in a sheet. It got my attention."

"And nothing's wrong with the painting? No damage?"

"Nothing wrong at all."

"Nothing except Annabel shouldn't have it."

"She doesn't."

Henry had taken the painting to Bib's to hide, but Bib was out of jail and didn't want more trouble, so Henry trekked along the river to the boathouse and left it there, intending to come back the next day after he'd decided on somewhere safer to stash it. I enjoyed the irony of secreting "my cock" in the darkness, where Annabel and I had shared moments of carnal satisfaction.

Perhaps I should have given the situation more thought. Neva, the lunch waitress, had brought my grilled cheese and chips, when Buck sat down at my table. "Don't object to my joining you, do you?" he asked, as if I had a choice. He took off his hat, laid it on the empty chair, and ordered a Nehi soda. "Good time of year, autumn coming on," he said, and inquired about school starting and what kind of football team the Academy would have this year. Neither of us predicted a winning season. Instead of Neva, Ruth brought the sheriff's soda—professional courtesy. She was too busy to linger and chat.

Buck wasn't too busy to talk to me. In fact, he was at the café to do just that. I sensed the topic might be more serious than autumn foliage, football, and hunting season. He drank his soda quickly. I had taken a few bites of my sandwich. "Let's go," he said, as if he had run out of patience.

He stood up. I stood up. Neva came over. Buck told her I'd settle my bill later.

Buck sat down. I sat down, in his office now. The deputy was on patrol, and Neva's sister, the dispatcher, was on her lunch break. I didn't need Buck to lift the sheet to know what was leaning against the filing cabinet. He did it anyway. The painting appeared as unharmed as Henry said it was.

"Now—" Buck picked up some papers from his desk, "you listed this picture among the items destroyed in your fire. For the moment, let's assume it was." He waved the papers in the air. I made out the name of the insurance company on the letterhead.

"Perhaps I assumed wrong. Perhaps I shouldn't have included the painting," I said.

"Oh, why not?"

"Because I was buying the painting from Annabel Spier and I owe her. Maybe she still owns it. But the bank still owns my house and it's insured."

"You have a mortgage. Any insurance settlement goes to the bank. Annabel said she didn't give you a bill of sale for the painting. Your handshake deal…—" Buck paused and raised his eyes to the ceiling, as if considering what other body parts may have been involved. He continued, "…Or whatever it was, isn't like buying a house." I shifted in my chair. The rooster's arrogant expression hadn't changed any. "I didn't figure you for someone who'd try to defraud anyone. I don't think your employer did either."

I was going to explain that whatever money the insurance company gave me for the painting I intended to hand over to Annabel, but there was no reason to drag things out. "No, sir," I said meekly.

"I've spoken to Miss Annabel. She's agreeable to writing the insurance company and explaining that you mistakenly believed you owned the painting, but that she is the owner and, unfortunately, she cannot file a claim because her policy only covers items in her store. We can tiptoe around the fact that the painting was elsewhere when the fire occurred. No reason to kick that dog and start it barking. Might bite you bad. You drop your claim and go about your business. Of course, you and I and Miss Annabel understand the situation."

The situation: Buck was doing me a favor and I'd owe him one, or several, and Annabel would be reunited with the rooster, who eyed me from the corner of the room, as if he understood more than I did. I was the birdbrain.

"However," Buck continued, "my duty is to write a report and keep it in my file." Buck timed his words to let "*my file*" sink in. "Someone might come around asking questions as to your character."

I offered a mild protest. I believed the painting was destroyed, and I believed I owned it.

"I know you see things that way."

"How do you see things?"

"Darkly."

"How can I improve your vision?"

"Miss Delia found the painting in her boathouse. Was it another one of your trespassing adventures puttin' it there? Or did you have help?" Buck picked up a pencil and touched the lead to his tongue, ready to write down the name I might offer.

"No, sir," I said.

"Care to surmise how the painting found its way to the boathouse?"

I cared to surmise why Delia had gone to the boathouse. It wasn't like her. The risk was Annabel finding the painting, not Delia. That's why Henry was going to move the painting the next day. "You said Delia found it?"

"Are you surprised?"

"She was never much interested in boats."

"Is that what you counted on?"

"These days I don't count on much of anything."

Buck tapped his pencil on his desk. "Miss Delia is considering whether to let the boathouse stand or tear it down. It's seen better days." Buck grinned. "So have you. I bet you miss that house of yours. Mr. Polk rents to about anybody. What's it like having Indians for neighbors? No war dances or nothing?"

"We get along," I said. "No dances."

Buck raised his eyes to the ceiling. "Used to be that everyone in town got along. I hope we can get back to those times." Buck lowered his gaze and stared me in the eye. "Son, you've had advantages. Don't throw them away."

Now I couldn't drive along Main Street without checking to see whether Annabel's business appeared open or not. If the shades weren't up and the shop looked closed, I'd cruise down the alley to see if her car was parked there. Any sign of her and I'd drive away. Even though I thought the coast was clear, I entered the café through the back door and sat in the corner, where I could see everyone coming down the street. This way, I could duck out if I had to. But Annabel caught on and left me a note. Of course, Ruth had read it before she handed it to me. *I need some in-and-out time.* I didn't want any with Annabel, and I didn't think she wanted any with me. I wondered what she had in mind.

"Better have another order of ribs," Ruth advised. "Annabel sounds primed for action. You'll need your strength."

Danielle showed up. I pushed the note into my pocket. Then Erskine arrived, and we all moved to a larger table. We talked about everything except the Spier sisters and recent local events, topics too loaded to discuss.

Annabel parked her car and slammed the door. She stood outside in the glow from my trailer, observing the sky. I could see Henry's face observing Annabel from his window. Her Capri pants showed off how much weight she'd lost, and her blouse, top buttons undone, where she hadn't lost any.

"May I come in?"

"You sure you want to?"

"Are you thinking of my feelings or yours?"

"Perhaps I wasn't thinking at all."

"I've been known to affect men that way."

Mr. Polk provided each trailer with a wooden set of steps. I stood on the ground, admiring the thrust of Annabel's hips. She pushed the screen open and I followed her inside.

"Guess you don't have to worry about getting lost." Annabel looked the trailer up and down. "You have running water?" I pointed to the sink. Annabel pointed to her blouse. "I spilled Coke on myself driving over here."

She stood close to me. Her breath let me know she'd been drinking something stronger than Coke.

"You need a sponge or something?"

"A towel."

I found a clean one in the basket of laundry Henrietta had washed for me. When I turned around, Annabel had removed her blouse and was holding the sleeve under the faucet.

"You're staring, Finn. I'm not sure if I should be annoyed or flattered." She turned off the water and shook out her blouse.

"You can't wear it wet," I said.

"I don't intend to. You're going to loan me a shirt."

I found one for her. She held it up and sniffed. "Rinso," she said. "I always liked your smell better. Does Danielle like it?"

"I don't know."

"Do you like hers?"

"I never thought about it."

"You're a poor liar, Finn. Or a poor lover. Which would you rather be?"

"I didn't mean to lie about the painting."

"But you did."

"I thought you sold it to me."

"And the insurance company thought you lost it the fire."

"I thought I had."

"But you hadn't."

"No."

"Your conclusion?"

"Someone saved it."

"A mysterious passer-by who raced into the flames, rescued the lovely fowl, and returned it to a boathouse safe and sound? That's a much better story than you setting the fire yourself and there being no paintin' to burn up 'cause you put it someplace else."

Even Buck hadn't suggested that I had started the fire. "Why would I burn down my house?"

"Insurance. Money. You just didn't have the heart to burn the cock, and I bless you for your concern. I'm delighted to have him back."

No point in bringing Henry into things, his finding the painting in Stony's garage. Annabel tilted her head and arched her brow, enjoying my stunned silence. She wasn't finished. "Buck asked me how you could afford to buy a house in the first place on what you make at the school. I told him Belle helped you out."

"I hope the sheriff hasn't given up trying to find who did set the fire."

"He warned you, didn't he, about upsetting the community, admitting a Negro to the Academy?" I nodded. So did Annabel. "You're not stupid, Finn, though sometimes you pretend you are."

"What are you saying?"

"Buck provides you cover. You do what Buck warns you someone else might do. Belle had put down half of what the house cost. The insurance comes through. The bank gets paid. You keep the rest. You walk away with a few hundred dollars, live in a trailer for a while, maybe sleep at Danielle's. Not like living at Red Sticks, but not too uncomfortable either."

"I appreciate your stopping in for a visit. Without a television or a radio, I don't have much entertainment."

"I'm not here to amuse you, Finn."

"Your note suggested passion."

"Somewhere on my way here I came to my senses."

"I'm sure we both have."

"Finn, I'll be watching."

"I'm sure we both will."

I hadn't been watching what Henry was up to. However, I was aware from the sweep of lights across our trailers that Buck or his deputy had paid us a couple of visits during the night. In the morning Henrietta stopped by and told me that Henry wanted to see me at Bib's. I should bring the key Mr. Sill had found in the jacket.

Henry and Bib were sitting on his porch. Bib and I had never been formally introduced. I shook his hand—bony fingers and calloused skin. He wore his army dog tags on a string around his neck. His teeth indicated a fondness for chewing tobacco. He offered me some, and I declined. If Buck had wondered how I could afford a house, I wondered how Bib could.

He went inside to fetch a deer antler he wanted to show us. When he came back and passed it around, I asked him.

"I do a bit of this and a bit of that, enough to get by, but I couldn't afford this property except I got it free. The cabin used to be nicer. This land was part of the judge's. He'd bring women here. Did it for years. He paid well. Some of them were rough characters from Burke City and as far away as Charleston. Finally Belle had enough. To patch things up, the judge agreed to quit any claim to the cabin and the land it's on. Before the war I'd helped some at the house. The judge liked me. I was home on leave, and Belle was impressed I'd made corporal. I seemed like the right man to own the cabin. After the war I moved in. I used to work steady, but I got lazy, I guess."

"And thirsty," Henry added.

"Indeed, it is so," Bib said.

Henry asked if I'd brought the key. "Most of the house is like it was when the judge visited, but one night Buck came out looking for Bib and kicked the door in."

"The old one's under the porch," Bib said.

Henry told me to crawl under there and pull out the part of the old door with the lock, and see if the key fit.

They chuckled at my lack of enthusiasm. I kept my head down, my face almost in the dirt. I inched over rotted boards and boxes, pushing bottles and pieces of glass out of the way with the remains of a broom without a handle. I saw the door. I bent my arm, keeping my elbow on the ground for leverage, and raised the door up, exposing what I took to be two feet of brown rope. The rope coiled into a copperhead. Henry and Bib had been squatting down, commenting on my progress and offering advice. I didn't move.

"Finn, you all right?"

I wanted to answer Henry, but I couldn't. I wanted to let go of the door, but I couldn't.

"Finn?"

"Found one," I heard Bib say.

Henry had spoken of experiencing the heat from Annabel's body. I felt the heat from his. He moved so silently I didn't hear him, but I could feel his heat and his presence. Then he was beside me. A sound left his throat. A hum, a chant, rolling and smooth and soothing. The snake uncoiled slowly and curved its way into the darkness, deep under the cabin. Henry helped me tug the door loose and drag it into the light.

Bib took the key. The lock was rusted and only the tip of the key went in. Bib spit on it and slid it back and forth. The key went in more each time. Then all the way. The lock turned.

"You're not surprised, are you? I said.

Henry glanced at Bib, then looked at me. Now was the time to tell me what he'd been not telling me. I wasn't figuring things out on my own. "No. I'd seen your momma wearing that fur thing before," Henry said.

Bib placed the key in my palm. "I saw her wearing it, too. I was home on leave, Christmas nineteen hundred forty-three. You know how Doc Spender always threw a party, a real big one. I was earning some extra money washing dishes. Your momma was carrying around trays and things. She'd come to work wearing the jacket over her uniform. One of the other women helping out called her stuck up and suggested how your momma came by the jacket and what she could do with it. Your momma and her got to shoving each other until the cook pulled 'em apart. After the party was over and the cleaning up was done, the jacket was missing. Your momma searched all over, but it was gone. The girl she'd been fightin' was still there, but the jacket wasn't."

Whoever took the jacket wore it to the club. There was a party there, too. Bib said it lasted until dawn. Whoever wore the jacket to the club didn't wear it home. Buck's father was sheriff then. That morning, five county residents driving away from the club had ran off the road or crashed into trees. Half a dozen service men passed out in their cars. Buck's father, with the blessing of the military, shut the club down. The bank had called in its note. The club was bankrupt anyway.

What could I say? They studied me the way you look at someone who has touched a hot wire, been jolted by an electric current, watching to see how that person will react, but not expecting him to say anything. I didn't try.

I started walking toward my car. Henry caught up with me, told me he wouldn't be around for a while.

Danielle had some Kentucky whiskey from a trip she took there last year. One look at me and she decided it was a time to open the bottle. We took the pieces of the summer apart and tried to put them together again into a pattern that meant something, that revealed something. When we didn't do very well with the summer, we worked our way to a more distant past. Pieces were missing, or we didn't know how to fit together the ones we had.

Danielle invited me to stay over. She didn't want me driving into any ditches or trees. All we did was to lie side-by-side holding hands. I'm not sure who fell asleep first, but she was awake before I was. I squeezed oranges while she warmed some muffins and made coffee. Her kitchen was yellow and cheerful and nearly as wide as my whole trailer. And there was a phone.

I dialed Spender's office and told the receptionist I wanted an appointment— "a vision problem," I said. Big Spender was cutting back, working half days. He was booked through the morning. I could have an appointment with Stony. She asked how much I could see. "Shapes," I said, "but details are unclear." Big Spender could work me in tomorrow morning.

On my way to a teachers' meeting, I saw Father Chester leaving the town library with an armful of books. I stopped and offered him a ride. The weather had heated up again. He mopped his brow and thanked me.

"When you kindly returned the photograph, I forgot to mention that one morning Annabel came to the church with Delia. Mrs. Twain gave Annabel a duster and set her to work on my library. Every now and then we make a passable try at spring-cleaning, though this was summer. I think Annabel spent more time complaining than dusting, but some of the books interested her. I found her sitting on the floor in the corner of my office with her knees tucked up, perusing an art book. Can't recall which one. I had to ask her to pull her dress down." Father Chester pressed his handkerchief to his cheek. "She was quite developed for her age. I guessed it wouldn't be many years until the local swains would make the opposite request, and whether she did or didn't comply, she'd give it some thought."

I parked by the church office. "You mean it wasn't the request, but who made it that mattered to her?"

Father Chester pressed the books against his chest and pushed the door open with his other arm. "Gracious, my tongue is wagging today. I apologize."

"Finish your thought," I said.

"Finn, I think I've said enough for you to finish it for me."

I waited near the oak shading Big Spender's Cadillac. He came out the back door, dressed in white trousers and a green polo shirt. He opened the trunk and took out a pair of golf shoes, tapping the spikes against each other, loosening some dried grass that drifted across the parking lot.

"Tomorrow won't suit you?"

"The impatience of youth," I responded.

"A vision problem, according to the note I received?"

"The past. Things aren't too clear there."

He looked at me warily. "What things?"

"Did you send my mother to Indianapolis?"

"Do you believe I did?"

"Yes."

"You're right. I did."

"You sent pregnant women to Indianapolis."

"To a man I trusted. We were in medical school together. For personal reasons, his career didn't prosper, but that didn't affect his qualifications. I sent patients to him for his advice. I'm not privy to what he advised them to do. You understand?"

I understood Spender was protecting himself. "You sent your girls, someone said."

"My girls?"

"I think he meant women who worked at the Shilling Club."

"I offered my assistance to any and all who asked for it."

"Do you remember when the club opened?"

"I'm not sure it ever did. It sort of emerged. During Prohibition, one of the local hunters had a property with an abandoned garage and an old house behind it. He'd get together with his friends and neighbors after a day in field or forest to swap stories, listen to a football game on the radio, and fortify weary bones with whatever fermented products had been, by whatever means, acquired. Prohibition ended, but the drinking continued. Then the property was sold, and the new owner fixed it up and offered memberships. He wore an old coin with a hole in it on a silver chain. He said the coin was a pine tree shilling from colonial times in Massachusetts."

"What did the club offer?"

"Young Finn, you're old enough to figure that out. Besides, I'm late."

"I need to know more."

"All of us do."

Spender took a monogrammed key case from his pocket. He invited me to ride and talk. We pulled out of the parking lot. "The sheriff knew about the club?"

"As much as he wanted to know. Money changed hands."

"You said before you weren't a member."

"I was given honorary status."

"What about the judge?"

"Timon? He never went there, though I believe he lent an attentive ear to stories about the place."

"And Georgia, my mother?"

"I have very little knowledge of her life."

"But you sent her to Indianapolis."

"She wrote me a postcard. She praised the scenery."

We passed the café and Annabel's shop. In front of the church, Father Chester was standing on the grass, observing something in the sky, or perhaps beyond it. I hoped so. I looked at the road ahead. The ride was smooth. The car was nicely appointed. Spender had gotten what he paid for.

I said, "I was born in nineteen thirty-four."

"Sounds right to me. I brought you into this world. Are you asking a question?"

Spender was being obscure about chronology. "Was my mother one of your girls?"

"No, she was not."

We turned onto the road to the cemetery and the golf course. I wondered how I was going to get back to my car.

"When you sent my mother to Indianapolis, you didn't expect what would happen."

"She praised the scenery and returned home."

"In the same condition she left."

"Your questions all sound like statements."

"They are."

"Yes, she returned to Blue County in the condition she left it."

I doubted Georgia could afford to travel out of state. I wondered who paid for her trip, if he got his money's worth. I inquired. Spender didn't answer. He turned into the driveway that ended at the club. I inquired again. "Your mother's finances were none of my concern." He shut off the motor. "You should take up golf. Clears the mind, relaxes the body. You see things better. Long walks are good, too," he added.

I wandered back to the road. Instead of setting off downhill, I walked the opposite direction, to the cemetery, where generations of Spiers were buried. The family considered the ground at Red Sticks too close to the river to bury the dead there, after a flood during the Revolution had raised several coffins and floated them away. I admired Calendar Spiers' memorial: balanced on a marble base, an opened book, the copper pages covered by a dark patina. During the long years of the war, when wounded Confederate troops came and went from Red Sticks, she wrote letters home for those who could not write and amused herself composing couplets. One was inscribed on the pedestal under the book: Here my bones may be, But not the rest of me.

I found Caroline, returned from England, standing by Belle's grave, holding a tin can of poppies.

She kissed my cheek. "Dear Finn, I hear your summer has not been restful."

"Not altogether. Yours?"

"Very." She smiled like someone in love. "You. should stop in and meet Franny, Lady Frances."

"I don't think your sisters would appreciate my presence."

"They're not inviting you. I am."

"Will I need a bullet-proof vest?"

"Oh Finn, don't be difficult." Caroline bent down, took the poppies from the can, and arranged them in the flower cup at the foot of Belle's grave. "Belle would have liked Franny."

"As much as you do?"

Caroline glanced at me over her shoulder. She poured water from the can onto the poppies and stood up.

"Belle would have understood. In fact—well, never mind."

I thought I knew what Caroline was thinking. "Belle and Timon, someone remarked theirs was not a marriage made in heaven."

"It was an appropriate marriage, socially, economically, those sorts of things. Belle understood what the cost would be. She didn't misunderstand her husband's character, only her own. However, if she had understood herself sooner, the cost might have been unbearable."

"I think I know what we're talking about."

Caroline put her arm around mine. "Don't say it, Finn. I don't like those words."

Caroline was puzzled why I had no car and no way home. I told her that Spender had prescribed exercise, but a ride was more to my liking. I gave her directions to my trailer. On the way, I asked what she knew about Mrs. Evening.

"Nothing." Caroline spoke sharply. She stared ahead.

"You know something," I said, softly.

"We all know something."

"What was her name?" Caroline shook her head. "You don't know, or you won't tell me?"

"You have no need to know."

"Let's change the subject."

"Yes, let's do."

"Names of other women the judge expressed an interest in?"

"You don't have to be delicate on my account."

"Perhaps it's on my account. One of the women was my mother."

"Yes, she was. After you moved to Red Sticks, I overheard Belle make a rather heated reference to my father and your mother. Of course, Belle knew about the others and eventually stopped caring, but your mother's case was different. Belle cared. I don't know why."

"Perhaps Mrs. Evening does."

"No, she doesn't."

"I'd like to find that out for myself."

"I have no idea where she is."

"Where did she used to be?"

Caroline stopped the car. "I don't know. I never did. She came and went."

"What did you think?"

"What Belle told us. The woman was a nurse. She worked late at the hospital in Burke City. From time to time, she stopped in to see Timon, to bring him something to help him sleep. She used the fire stairs. We never saw her, only the Plymouth she drove.

"Never?"

Caroline hesitated and took a deep breath. "All right. Delia was in France. Annabel was outside smoking a cigarette. She didn't think a nurse would show up in a cocktail dress and high heels, but we kept our thoughts to ourselves. Eventually Belle told us the truth. She was very careful how she said it. By that time, Mrs. Evening no longer visited, and Timon needed real nursing. What did you think?"

"It wasn't any of my business. Belle said from time to time Timon had a visitor. I stayed in my room the way Belle told me to and did my homework, or fell asleep."

Caroline was silent for a moment. I must not have sounded convincing. She picked at a thread on her skirt. "Finn, I know you. You're not telling me everything."

"Sometimes I'd sneak out. One night I saw the head-lights of the Plymouth just before the driver switched them off. She sat in the car for a while, like she was thinking about something. Then she stepped away from the car and pulled a coat around her. I hunkered behind the camellias. She passed close to me. I never saw her face, but I remembered the way she walked. Something was wrong with one of her legs."

Caroline nodded. Our conversation was over. When Caroline let me out, she asked me to bring Henry along to meet Franny. An Indian would fascinate her. Maybe he would tell us what he had thrown into Belle's grave. I said that Henry was away.

Enough whiskey left for two drinks. Danielle and I sipped them and watched the sun go down. It wasn't the summer we tried to take apart and put together this time, only what Spender and Caroline had told me. Who did I think paid my mother's way to Indianapolis? Spender himself? The judge? Danielle voted for the judge. I agreed, mostly because we didn't have other candidates.

Georgia had gone to Indianapolis pregnant and returned pregnant. Whoever sent her probably wasn't pleased. She bore a child. "You?" Danielle asked.

I remembered the afternoon Tyrone left. "Going on a little trip," he said. "Overnight to Wilmington." He'd packed a small suitcase with a strap around it. We sat on the front steps while he waited for his ride. "Finn…" He took off his hat and wiped the brim. Then he put his hat back on and adjusted it low over his eyes. "You remind me of how happy your mother and I used to be," he said. He found his sunglasses, put them on, and wiped his cheek, like he was sweating, but I think he was crying. His ride appeared, someone's truck. A tarp covered the back, so I don't know what the truck was hauling, or if it was going to Wilmington or someplace else. In any case, I never saw Tyrone again.

"No," I said to Danielle. "No, Tyrone was my father. I'm sure of it. Georgia had another child before she had me."

SIX

School started. My freshmen grumbled about reading *Julius Caesar,* my sophomores about reading *The Merchant of Venice,* my juniors about reading *Hamlet,* my seniors about reading *Macbeth.* The new poetry anthology arrived, more American writers than British ones.

Twice I'd spent the night sleeping beside Danielle. The second time we'd made love. I woke up before dawn, listening to her breathing, listening to her mumble in her dreams. I had never spent the night with Annabel or the couple of girls I had sex with in college. Sleeping beside someone else was mysterious. Danielle looked peaceful and vulnerable at the same time. She knew things we'd never speak about. Secrets. I wanted to peer inside her and find them out. But, of course, I couldn't and would have been afraid to if I could. I slipped my hand under her shirt. She woke. We made love again.

I still didn't have a phone. I'd given the school's number to people who might call me. I'd written it down on Miss Polis's pad in case Mr. Tallmadge wanted to tell me something else.

She phoned the school and left a message. Pneumonia again. This time Mr. Tallmadge had died. I didn't have afternoon classes, so I could go to the funeral without finding someone to teach for me. Danielle didn't know Mr. Tallmadge, but lots of people who ran the county, or used to, would attend the funeral, so she decided to go with me.

The church was crowded and hot. We sat near the back. The double doors were open. Puffs of air drifted inside. Almost all the men seated in front of us had gray hair, or none at all. The women wore hats, all but a few. A mourner came late. I moved over to give her room. She wore a hat, too. I guessed she was fifty or fifty-five, years younger than Mr. Tallmadge. I wondered how she knew him. She opened her purse and took out a handkerchief. When we were invited to come forward for bread and wine, she left her purse open. She went up the aisle to the altar first. I told Danielle to go behind her. I looked into the purse: cigarettes, compact, a wallet. I took it out. The name on her driver's license was Marlene Gibbs.

Danielle returned from the front of the church. As she squeezed past me, she whispered, "What were you doing?" and sat down. Marlene sat down on the other side of me. Minutes later the casket was lifted and carried outside.

Marlene didn't linger to speak with anyone. I followed her to her car. The sound of her heels on the sidewalk, the way she walked stopped me in my tracks. I called out "Marlene?" She turned around.

"Lester spoke a lot about you," I said.

"How did you know him?" Marlene asked.

"He advised me about some unfinished business."

She looked me in the eye as if she didn't believe me, then

her expression softened. She almost smiled. "You're Finn, aren't you?"

"Can we talk?"

"I'm not sure we should."

Danielle was standing on the lawn watching us. The hearse waited in the street. A man was lining up cars to follow it. A trooper on a motorcycle was ready to lead it.

"How did you know my name?"

"I was at Belle's service, in the back. Someone pointed you out. How did you recognize me?"

I offered a reasonable answer. "Lester showed me your photograph." I didn't want to mention her walk.

The trooper revved his motor and started off. Marlene said something, but I couldn't hear her. I glanced toward the church. Danielle was sitting on a bench under one of the oaks.

"I don't think so," Marlene said. "He didn't have one."

"Then I'm not sure," I said.

"I am. When I was eleven, I fell out of a tree and broke my leg. It never healed like it should have. You know that from Red Sticks."

"I have lots of questions," I said.

"And you think I have lots of answers?"

"I think you have some."

"Finn, okay, but not here."

"Where?"

"I'd like to see Red Sticks again."

Only a few cars remained at the curb. I opened the driver's door of Marlene's Dodge. She used to own a Plymouth. She'd traded up. She hesitated. "Aren't you going to follow me?"

"I came with someone else."

Marlene looked around. "The woman on the bench?"

I said, "Yes," closed the door, and walked around to the passenger's side.

In the rearview mirror, Marlene watched Danielle stand up and start across the grass toward her car down the street. "She walks the way I wanted to," Marlene said. A few blocks later, Marlene asked me to light a cigarette for her. I'd find one in her handbag. "Of course you already know that," she said.

I shook one from the pack and pressed in the lighter. When it popped out, I touched the glowing coil to the tip of her Kent, puffed, and handed her the cigarette. "I saw what smoking did to Timon. I should quit, but it's hard."

"You expected me to look at your license, didn't you?"

Marlene smiled to herself. "Mrs. Evening, isn't that what Belle called me?"

I said it was. We were out of town now. Cattle lifted their heads as Marlene drove past. She had taken off her hat, the window was open, and the breeze loosened her hair. I could see why Lester had fallen for her. "Why don't you start," she said.

"Did you know my mother?" Marlene shook her head. "I knew about her."

"Did you know Doctor Spender?"

"Everyone did."

"He sent girls to Indianapolis. Did you know about that?"

Marlene leaned over and tapped her cigarette on the ashtray. "Girls from the club. Of course I knew."

"Did Spender pay for the girls to go?"

"He recommended travel, he didn't pay for it."

"I don't understand who gave my mother the money."

Marlene didn't speak. We passed a field of melons and a pasture with more cattle. Marlene put out her cigarette, pushed the ashtray shut, and rolled the window halfway up. "Finn, you deeply and truly want to know? Your world is going to change." She looked at me. I nodded yes. "Timon did. Timon paid," she said.

Now it was my turn not to speak. I opened the wing window and directed the air across my face. In a minute I closed it. The new sign was up: *Welcome to Sprite*. Finally I spoke, "Who was the child who wasn't supposed to be born?"

Marlene stared straight ahead, as if she hadn't heard me. Finally she spoke. "Finn, understand, I wouldn't be naming names except in some way I think, I hope, it will set things right. Others, naturally, will hold a different view, that I'm bitter and was never any good, that I don't live here anymore and just want to stir up trouble for those who do."

"Tell me," I said.

"Delia."

We drove through town and out the other side, into the country again, toward the river. A few minutes later, we stopped in front of Red Sticks. The gate was shut. If she honked her horn, someone might hear it and let us through.

"I can sit here and see what I want to see. A house divided," Marlene said.

I wasn't looking at the house. "Delia's my half-sister?"

"She is, but she doesn't know it."

Again, silence. I smelled the river and thought about Delia shooting at me, and how she was going to feel when she found out we were related, and who was going to tell her, if anyone did.

"The club closed. There was a fur jacket that no one claimed. Lester wanted to buy it for you, but Timon didn't let him."

"Poor Lester. He was gone on me. He offered to leave his wife and we'd disappear somewhere. I told him no. He was much more interested in me than I was in him. He was business. I didn't want to lead him on or away. His life was here."

"And yours wasn't?"

"For a while it was here."

"Tell me about the jacket."

"Timon gave your mother travel money and some extra guilt money, enough for her to treat herself to something expensive. When she came home carrying it and the child inside her, Timon was furious. But what could he do? He wanted the jacket. For a while, he offered a bounty, money to any of the girls at the club who could steal it and bring it to him. Then, what was she going to do about it? But he thought better of that idea. In fact he thought better of your mother. A few months after Delia was born…"

"Hold on. Where was Delia born? How did she get to be Belle's child without lots of other people knowing the truth?"

"Spender knew. Of course, he would, but no one else did. Timon told Belle about your mother. Belle hadn't been able to have a child. No one could see that your mother was going to have one, at least not yet. She moved into Red Sticks. The servants then were getting on in years and had talked about returning to their home place in Louisiana. Belle paid them seven months of wages, and they left. Belle would phone the market. Orders would be set by the back door. When it was time, Spender was called, and Delia was born at Red Sticks.

Spender wrote Belle's name on the birth certificate. New servants were hired, but they didn't last. Eventually Belle hired Simon and Asia, I imagine to the great relief of everyone. Belle could cook and run Red Sticks by herself, but Timon probably wasn't much help. According to Belle, he sulked for months. He was accustomed to giving orders, not taking them. After your mother left Red Sticks, Belle ordered Timon to keep away from her. That's an order he didn't have the good sense to take. Something about her he hadn't had enough of. They started visitin' each other again. The old cabin was convenient. Your mother had the good sense not to wear the jacket much, except the few winter nights when it's chilly enough to put on something like that. I saw her wearing it once at the club, but she didn't go there much either.

"Someone finally did steal it."

"Dot Surry. She never got on with your mother. I was at the club when Dot arrived from the Spender's shindig wearing the jacket, the last night at the club, although we didn't know it at the time. Ol' Dot ended up drunk and went off with some soldiers. I don't believe she intended to keep the jacket, only hoped to cause your mother to hunt around to find it. The next day, Dot probably didn't remember what she'd done, or didn't want to. She'd thrown the jacket into the rafters of the shed where ice was stored in the old days. Nasty place, full of spiders and broken furniture. She probably went there with one of her soldiers. Maybe he pitched it. In the end, someone checked to see if any of the stuff was worth selling, and found the jacket. It was there for the money, and Timon was willing to pay."

I told Marlene where the jacket was now. She laughed.

A school bus stopped behind our car and let Tunisia out.

The bus drove away, leaving a plume of diesel fumes in its wake. Tunisia said, "Hey." She could ask someone to open the gate. Marlene and I looked at each other. "We're just sight-seeing," I said. I watched Tunisia slip though the space between the gate and the gatepost. The shadows of the oaks filled the driveway. Tunisia stopped and turned around, studied us, then turned back toward the house.

Marlene inquired about Henry. She liked him. He'd been sweet to all the girls at the club. And they'd been sweet to him. I said I liked him, too.

Marlene leaned over, pressed the latch, and opened the glove box. She reached in and took out a pint of whiskey.

"One for the road?"

She unscrewed the top and passed me the bottle. I took a drink and handed the bottle to her.

"My road, I guess. I imagine you'll be here again. I won't be." She drank. "More?" I shook my head. She closed the bottle. I returned it to the glove box and shut the door. She started the car and backed away from the gate.

"Ironic," Marlene said. "After Delia, Belle had no trouble getting pregnant."

"And Belle told you what you've been telling me?"

Marlene regarded me with a sad look, the way Belle looked me over when I said I didn't know about the River Styx, and she said I had a lot to learn.

"Mrs. Evening was never here to visit Timon," Marlene said.

Yes, I had a lot to learn.

"What about Delia?" Danielle asked. "Think she'll believe anything you say?"

"I'm not sure if I will say anything."

"I think you should, Finn."

"If I talk to Delia, then what? What's changed? What's going to happen? I don't imagine Delia will invite me to move back to Red Sticks."

"Do you want to?"

"Trailer living agrees with me."

"More like you're living here."

"Here agrees with me."

"With me, too."

The wind rustled the leaves. In a few minutes, rain pattered on the roof. Danielle pulled the sheet over us. I pressed my mouth against her skin. I didn't want to talk anymore or listen to anything but the rain and Danielle's breathing next to me.

In the morning, the yard smelled of gasoline. Nothing caught fire because of the rain. Danielle said she'd phone Buck, for all the good it would do.

In the middle of October, Stony Spender was named to the Academy's board of trustees. At its first meeting, Dr. Curry expressed the wish of a majority of the faculty that the school continue its efforts to recruit a minority student, more than one if possible. Dr. Curry read a letter from William Polk recommending Marcellus Rainey. The Raineys farmed twenty acres a few miles out of town. During the winters, Mr. Polk hired Mr. Rainey to repair roofs and do some carpentry proj-

ects on his properties. Marcellus often accompanied his father. The boy was an avid reader and quick at math. Mr. Polk
recommended him highly. Stony was heard to grumble that
Bill Polk didn't know shit from Shinola. Stony's request for
a list of the faculty who favored admitting a Negro would be
addressed by Dr. Curry in private. Whether he gave Stony a
list or not, the faculty didn't know. We did learn, however, that
Albert agreed to reapply for admission if Marcellus applied. I
still had no idea where he had disappeared to during the summer. I asked Ella a couple of times. Once she pretended not to
hear me. The next time she said, "Let it lay."

Early one November morning, someone shot holes in the
Raineys' mailbox. "Disaffected youth," in Buck's opinion.
Yes, lots of disaffection going around. Danielle was the first
to notice how frequently Stony's truck was parked late into the
evening in the alley at Annabel's back door. Moving inven-
tory? We doubted it. Henrietta was acquainted with the maid
who worked for Stony and his wife. She told Henrietta that
Mrs. Spender had packed and left to visit her sister in Florida
and wasn't expected to return before Thanksgiving, if then.

Fired destroyed the Raineys' henhouse. "Faulty wiring to
the brooder lights," in Buck's opinion. Mr. Rainey wasn't using
brooder lights in November. "Lights don't have to be on for
wires to touch and spark," Buck said. Chief Sweeten pointed
out that gasoline was a contributing factor. "Farm people are
careless with flammables," Buck opined. Mr. Rainey wisely
declined to comment.

Thanksgiving week, a deer hunter found a body in the

scrub pines at the edge of the Raineys' farm. School was out for the holiday. I was inside, grading papers. I saw the deputy's car stop near Henrietta's trailer. I knew it was a sympathy call because the deputy removed his hat and held it in his hand when Henrietta let him inside. Three or four minutes later he left, and she knocked on my door. She raised her apron and wiped her eyes. Henry was dead.

She explained that Henry had been doing what he did in autumn, living in the woods the way his ancestors had, surviving on rabbits and squirrels, or the fish he caught in the river, or waterfowl he killed in the marsh. The deputy said Henry had been shot. Buck didn't want Henrietta to see the body until they carried it to the morgue in the basement of the county hospital in Burke City. "Better to visit after the coroner's finished and neatened up," the deputy said. County coroner was an appointed position. Big Spender had filled it for twenty years. The extra money brought him fog lights and chrome doodads for his Cadillacs. He would autopsy the body and write a report. No question, though, according the deputy, who the victim was and that he'd been shot. Once, in the back, it appeared.

We sat on Danielle's front steps, bundled up in sweaters, passing a jar of strong tea back and forth. Danielle had bought a turkey to cook, but a celebration didn't fit our mood. She contributed the bird to the Sisters of Fatima in Burke City, who fed whoever needed a meal, and provided a place to be on Thanksgivings and Christmases. I cooked beans and rice.

For once Buck's speculation was plausible. Another hunter had mistaken Henry's movement in the bushes for a deer's. "A man living like that, moving like an animal, keeping to shadows, obscured by branches and leaves—that's invitin' trouble. He was even wearing a deer suit." By which Buck meant that Henry had on deerskin trousers and a deerskin shirt. The Keds on his feet weren't exactly what his ancestors would have worn, but Henry was fond of the shoes, and probably found them better for his purposes than ones he could make himself out of hides.

By Wednesday morning Big Spender had finished his work. "Pretty routine," he said. That afternoon I drove Henrietta to the hospital and stayed in the car while she went inside and said goodbye to her brother. Henry's clothes and personal effects were returned to her: his rifle, his knife, a buffalo nickel, and a lanyard—strips of corded deerskin with a bear claw at one end.

She arranged the items on her lap. I asked her about the coin. She explained that Henry liked the nickels, considered them lucky. He liked to attend burials and drop one in the grave. It annoyed people, and he liked that, too. My people had annoyed plenty of his. But his purpose was the ancient one of offering the dead a gift to accompany the spirit on its journey to its next world.

Henrietta hadn't seen the lanyard for years. Henry had only made one, as far as she knew. There was something sacred about the bear claw. She wondered if Henry had taken it with him because he sensed his own dying. What did I think?

I said that I thought Henry had always sensed his own dying. I did not tell Henrietta what he had told me, how he had exchanged it for a favor from Annabel. I knew how Henrietta felt about her. She didn't need to find out that her brother had seen Annabel in a different light, at least once upon a time.

The fatal bullet was locked in Buck's safe. Danielle had read Spender's findings. The bullet had entered through the victim's back and exited near his heart. What caliber the bullet was, or what sort of gun fired it, those details were in Buck's province. We could speculate all we wanted to about the proximity of the shooter and the deceased, and what the shooter knew or didn't know, and why the shooter didn't report the accident, if that's what it was. If Buck were covering something up, we couldn't be sure. Of course, he would show the bullet to anyone who had a legal reason to see it. No one offered one. Eventually the bullet would disappear into the clutter of the sheriff's office and be forgotten.

Then there was the matter of Henry's camp, which the deputy had discovered in the pines. Others had apparently walked right by the place and seen nothing. Along with a lean-to and a fire pit, under a canvas was a gasoline can, almost empty, something from the white world that Henry would never have taken with him, but it made him look guilty of having something to do with Mr. Rainey's henhouse.

I told Danielle about Henry and Annabel, and the lanyard he made for her. "More questions than answers," Danielle said. "She hugged her knees, rested her chin on her arm, and asked what I was thinking about.

"Annabel and Stony," I said, but I didn't know what to say next.

The Academy played football on Friday afternoons. The school couldn't afford lights for the field. Thirty was a crowd.

Mostly parents, people stood on the sidelines in good weather, or sat in their cars near the sidelines when the wind blew rain.

A blue, early December sky. Crisp, but a tolerable temperature. The last game of the season, always against a county-day school from Burke City. Erskine's grandson was quarterback. He'd thrown a pass to Tracy's nephew, and the game was tied at halftime.

Grinning, Tracy shook my hand. I'd stopped at his office, but he'd been out of town. "What's on your mind?" he said.

We walked toward the goal line, away from parents and the others.

"The Shilling Club, the token you gave me."

"Did it bring you luck?"

"I'm not sure yet. And I'm not sure if Belle thought it would."

"Belle?"

"She saved it for me."

"Are you asking me to confirm that?"

"You don't have to."

A cheer went up. The teams were returning to the field.

Tracy put his hand on my shoulder. "My nephew tells me about the poets you assign, new ones. Robinson, is that one of them?"

"E. A. Robinson, yes, and others."

"I don't know, Finn, but I think young men like reading Robert Service or Sidney Lanier, the older poets. Or Alfred Noyes. I memorized most of 'The Highwayman' when I was in school. "

"Robinson isn't new," I said.

"New to me. New to most of us here."

"Towns need new things—buildings, poets, sometimes new doctors and law officers."

"I suppose you've heard that Stony Spender is taking a position in Mississippi."

"And you may be handling his divorce."

"Sad but true, young Finn."

"I've also heard that Annabel Spier is going out of business."

"She's young. Good for her to get away."

"I couldn't agree more."

"She'll find her place somewhere."

"Perhaps she already has."

Big Spender decided to forego his traditional Christmas party, but Delia decorated Red Sticks with pine boughs, holly, and nandina berries, and gave a small one there.

The gate was open. Albert was outside directing people to parking places. Simon was inside taking coats and hats. In red velvet, Delia greeted her guests, many wondering how she managed to keep a dress cut so low from falling off. "One can always hope," Erskine said.

I left Danielle and walked through the kitchen, pausing to smell the roasts cooling on cutting boards and to sample the Yorkshire pudding that Franny had taught Asia how to make.

I used the back stairs. The door to my old room was open. A bright blanket covered the bed. Three books lay on the table, the one Tunisia had been reading and the one I had given her, and another one, a world atlas with Albert's name on the top corner of the title page: Albert Cates, July 1960.

Delia had followed me. "He forgot to take it with him," she said.

"He was here?"

"All the time. Po' Billy's sister clerks at the market. I started buying different groceries. Albert has a liking for chocolate milk and cookies. Billy came to see who I was feeding. Might be the boy people were looking for."

"I'm sorry. I had no idea."

"I learned from Belle how to lead two lives at once and hide feelings in plain sight. But I'm just learning how much was out of sight."

"Who have you been talking to?"

"Henry, when he stopped by to see Annabel. And Tracy."

"Henry?"

"He came for Annabel, but she wasn't here. Henry told me to tell her where he was camping. He'd given her something and he wanted to know if she still had it. He didn't say what it was."

"Did Henry mention the Shilling Club?"

"He didn't. Tracy did."

"Where's Annabel now?"

"Caroline and Franny flew home to England. Annabel's gone to Biloxi."

There was a party downstairs and Delia needed to be there, but she waited for another question.

"When you helped Father Chester and Mrs. Twain at the church and Annabel came along, did you ever see the photograph of him she found?"

"I wish I hadn't. My mother saw it, too. She explained some things to me."

I told Delia where Danielle and I had found it.

Henrietta had let me keep Henry's nickel. I took it out and showed it to Delia. "Annabel liked Henry," I said.

"He knew things about her. She didn't like that." Delia took the coin out of my hand and studied it. "Henry came and went and we never saw him, but he saw us." She placed the nickel on my palm again.

"Saw us more than we knew," I said.

Delia rearranged the books on the table. "Finn, I recognized the jacket in the photograph. I found the jacket in my father's closet. Belle saw me try it on and had a fit."

I pocketed the nickel and took out the token. "Did you find this?"

"Belle did. She put it in an envelope with your name on it. I asked Tracy not to tell you."

"You need to get back to your guests," I reminded her.

She shook her head. "I remember when the judge told us you were going to be a guest and live here. He wanted a son. I didn't want a brother. I'm sorry for the way I was and, since Belle died, the way I had to be."

I didn't know Delia was well as I thought I did. But after the judge took me in, she was away most of the time. I didn't have much to go on. Now I was learning.

I squeezed Delia's hand. "Your other guests," I said.

I let myself out the back door. I stood in the night. I listened to the river flowing by. I thought I heard someone behind me and turned around, but no one was there.